Lords for the Sisters of Sussex Series

The Duke's Second Chance
  The Earl's Winning Wager
  Her Lady's Whims and Whimsies
  Suitors for the Proper Miss
  Pining for Lord Lockhart
  The Foibles and Follies of Miss Grace

Follow Jen's Newsletter for a free book and to stay up to date on her releases. https://www.subscribepage.com/y8p6z9

Follow Jen

Jen's other published books

The Nobleman's Daughter
Two lovers in disguise

Scarlet
The Pimpernel retold

A Lady's Maid
Can she love again?

His Lady in Hiding
Hiding out at his maid.

Spun of Gold
Rumplestilskin Retold

Dating the Duke
Time Travel: Regency man in NYC

Charmed by His Lordship

The antics of a fake friendship

Tabitha's Folly
Four over protective Brothers

To read Damen's Secret
The Villain's Romance

Follow her Newsletter

Chapter One

Morley stared at his best friend, waiting for the man to look up from his cards. Gerald was losing terribly. And Morley wasn't sure if he should feel guilty or victorious. His friend had just thrown most of a new inheritance from his distant cousin on the table, almost as if he wished to give it away.

Despite Gerald being the Duke of Granbury with significant holdings to his name, Morley wasn't comfortable taking so much —even in something as unbiased as a card game. But his friend smiled so large it looked like his cheeks hurt. Morley's hurt just looking at him.

"How can you smile when you're losing abominably?" Lord Morley frowned at him.

"I have leave to be happy so soon after my own wedding."

"But you don't have leave to gamble away your living, even to your best friend."

"I'm hardly close to losing a living."

Lord Morley raised his eyebrows. The other lords at the table stared greedily at the back of Gerald's cards. But even though Lord Morley shook his head, none too subtly, Gerald pushed all the remaining chips and his slips of paper into the center.

"Included in this are some holdings in the south."

Lord Morley narrowed his eyes.

Gerald fanned out his cards. "Good, but"—he smiled even broader—"not good enough." Then each of the men laid out their cards. Gerald beat Lord Oxley soundly, as Morley suspected he knew he would. Then Lords Harrington and Parmenter threw their cards down. That left Morley's cards. Morley had won. Gerald knew he'd won. He eyed him above his cards. "What is this about?"

"Lay out your cards, man. On with it." Gerald's smile couldn't grow any larger, and even though Morley had just grown significantly more wealthy, he didn't trust his oldest friend.

Morley fanned out his cards and narrowed his eyes. "What are you doing?"

Gerald tipped his glass back and drained its contents. "Losing to my best friend. Come now. It's time for us to return home. Her Grace wants me home early."

"How is she feeling?"

Gerald's face clouded, and Morley regretted the question. Since the man had lost his first wife during childbirth, the prospect of doing it all over again loomed in his mind at all hours. Morley talked to him of it often enough. "She seems in the very prime of health. No one has looked healthier."

"No need to speak optimism in my ear. I know she is well, but then, so was Camilla. All we can do is wait and see. Amelia so wanted a child, and I love my wife too much to leave her alone. So there we have it."

Morley clapped him on the back as they stepped out of White's. "Do you ever consider it odd that when youth, we used each other's titles in preparation for the moment the great weight would fall on our shoulders? And now. You still call me Morley, but I ... don't call you anything but Gerald." He laughed trying to lighten the mood.

"You will always be Morley. Even your mother calls you Morley." He laughed. "Why is that?"

"I couldn't guess. Maybe she loves the title?" He shrugged. "Now, enough mystery. Tell me, what did I just win? What's this all about? These holdings in the south?"

"Remember our visit to Sussex?"

Morley half nodded, and then he stopped dead in the street. "When we went to save you from Lady Rochester? And we paid a visit to a family of ladies?" His eyes narrowed. Unbidden, Miss Standish's face came into his mind. "What did you do?"

"I inherited their castle, if you recall."

"I recall a heap of rubble with a few standing rooms."

"Well, we've been fixing it up, and the ladies are just about ready to move in. Five women, all of age. June, the eldest, is not quite twenty three, the youngest sixteen. You won the whole lot of them, with some other holdings besides. The winnings should cover the remaining repairs and upkeep for a time as well."

"I won't take it."

"You have no choice. There were witnesses."

Morley was silent for so long he hoped Gerald began to half suspect he'd truly overstepped his generosity at long last. Then he shook his head. "I know what you're doing, and she doesn't want anything to do with me."

"I don't know what you're talking about."

"And she will want even *less* to do with me if she thinks she is in any way beholden to me, so whatever plans you have going, you can just take back your properties and your pesky family of women and leave me in peace."

"Morley, you're my oldest and best friend. Would I really foist these women on you if I didn't think it would make you the happiest of men? They're from the Northumberland line. Excellent family heritage. The Queen herself takes an interest in their well-being."

"I care not for any of such nonsense, and you know it. You are not to be a matchmaker. It doesn't suit you. And you're terrible at it."

3

"How would you know, since I've never attempted such a roll until now?"

"So you admit it?"

"I admit nothing. Now, come, don't be cross. You'll upset Amelia."

"Oh, that is low, bringing your wife's condition into this."

They stepped into the townhome, where Simmons took their hats and gloves and overcoats. Gerald waved Morley in. "Thank you for staying with us while you're in town."

"At times, I prefer your home to my own situation."

"You're a good son, though."

Morley hoped he was, though his mother was tiring at best and liked to have her fingers in most aspects of his dealings. He loved her, and felt she was happy in her life, such as it was.

A soft, melodic voice called, "Gerald? Is that you?"

Amelia stepped out into the foyer. "And Morley." She clapped her hands, and the smile that lit her face filled the room.

He accepted her kiss on the cheek and watched as Gerald turned all of his focus to his wife.

Morley bowed. "I will bid you good night. Tomorrow, Gerald, we will discuss your sneaking ways."

"What has he done?" Amelia could only look with love at the Duke, and Morley felt, for a moment, a pang of loneliness.

"I've done nothing. Morley is just a sore winner."

Morley refused to say more. He bowed to Amelia and made his way up the stairs. Before he reached the first landing, he turned. "Oh, and Gerald?"

Gerald turned from his wife for a brief moment.

"When are we to go visit my winnings?"

"Oh, you're on your own with that one, Morley. They will much prefer you to me at any rate." He turned back to Her Grace, and Morley continued up the stairs, his mood darkening with every step.

Gerald had gone too far—in some mad effort to match him with a woman who really had no more interest in Morley than she did dancing a quadrille. June Standish was as practical as he'd seen a person.

He sighed.

And far handsomer than any he'd yet laid eyes on. Her hair was gold—it looked to be spun from the metal itself—and her eyes large, doe-like. He had lost all sense of conversation when he first saw her. It had taken many minutes for him to gain his faculties enough to speak coherently, but she had seemed entirely unaffected. And so that was it for them.

He could only imagine her reaction when he returned to let her know a new gentleman, he himself, was now lord over her life and well-being. Gerald should not toy with others' lives. He needed to be stopped. But Morley wasn't going to be the one to stop him. They'd carried on in their friendship in just this way since they'd known each other. Perhaps he could appeal to Amelia. She had more control over the man than anyone.

What did he need with a decrepit, dilapidated castle? It was an old seat of the royal dukes, so there was a certain level of prestige associated with the place—and with the women. They were of the ancient Normandy family lines. Someone somewhere in their family had wasted their money and left nothing for the line to live off of, but it was still considered an elevated situation if you were on friendly terms with any of the Sisters of Sussex, as they were called.

Sleep did not come easily, and morning was not friendly to Morley's tired eyes and mind. Instead of breaking his fast with Gerald and Amelia, he left for a walk. Oddly, his steps took him to Amelia's old tearoom. They let it out, once she was to become the duchess, and someone else ran the establishment instead. As he stood in the doorway, he almost walked away without entering. What was he doing in a tearoom? Colorful dresses filled the shop to bursting.

"Lord Morley!" With the swish of skirts, a woman's hands were on his arm. "What a pleasant surprise. You must join us for tea. We are discussing the upcoming McAllister ball."

He allowed himself to be led to their table, and when four expectant female eyes turned their hopeful expression toward him, he could only smile and say, "How perfect, for I was just wondering about the details."

"Then you are attending?" Lady Annabelle's eyes lit with such a calculating energy, he shifted in his seat, eyeing the door for a second.

"I am, indeed."

"How provident. Then we shall all be there together. You remember we all became acquainted at the opera one week past. Miss Talbot, Miss Melanie—"

"And Lady Annabelle. Naturally, we are acquainted. It is a pleasure to see you again. I hope your mother is well?"

Lady Annabelle poured his tea, and his mind could not leave the family he'd just won charge of. What sort of women was this new family of sisters? He'd been most impressed with them when considering them as Gerald's wards, of a sort. But now that he owned the house they lived in, he felt a whole new interest in their deportment. Could they pour a man's tea? Stand up well with the other ladies at a ball? Would he be able to marry them off? That was the crux of it. And dash it all, why must he be concerned with the marrying off of anyone? He was in over his head. He needed help. He could appeal to Amelia's sense of grace, but she would have little knowledge of the ways of the *ton*.

The women chattered around him, and he almost sloshed his tea in the saucer when he heard mention of the very women who so aggravated his thoughts.

"They call them the Sisters of Sussex."

"Really? Who are they?"

"The Duke of Northumberland's relations, from a royal line. They are the talk of the *ton* and favorites of many of the noble families. We ourselves have stopped by with some of last season's gowns."

"Five sisters, you say? And they live in the old castle?"

"A cottage nearby. The castle is being renovated, though. I

heard the Duke of Granbury has become involved." Lady Annabelle turned to him. "Do you know much about the sisters?"

He cleared his throat and shifted in his seat. "I have met them."

The other ladies leaned forward, eyes on him.

"And I found them charming," he said. "I think you know more about their history than I. Though I do know the castle will be repaired and livable, as it deserves to be. It's a remarkable structure."

Miss Talbot fanned her face. "I should like to visit. I love old buildings and their architecture."

"Do you?" Morley tipped his head to her. She was a pretty sort of woman. Chestnut curls lined her face, and deep brown eyes smiled at him.

"Yes, I like to draw them, and then study them after."

"Interesting. Perhaps we shall meet up there sometime."

"Oh?" Lady Annabelle rested a hand on his arm. "Will you be spending much time in Brighton?"

He hadn't planned on it yet. He'd hoped to stay as far away as possible until his mind wrapped around this new responsibility. But he changed his plans in the moment. "I think I shall." He looked into each of their faces. They were pleasant women. They seemed kind—unassuming, perhaps. "Might I ask for some assistance?"

"Certainly." Lady Annabelle's eyes gleamed.

"I wonder, if I were to assist the ladies—any ladies—to be prepared for a smallish Season in Brighton, do they have a dressmaker or shops enough down there?"

"Oh, certainly. Not nearly as grand or varied as London, but a woman can make do with what Brighton has to offer. The Brighton Royal Pavilion has brought much of the *ton* and a higher level of prestige to the area."

"Thank you."

Their gossip-loving ears seemed to perk right up and all three pairs of eyes looked on him a bit too keenly. He resisted adjusting his cravat. "So, who will be attending the McAllister ball? And have each of you found partners already for your dances?"

The chatter grew more excited, and they listed all the people who were coming or might be coming, depending on the attendance of others. He lingered as long as was polite, and then excused himself from this cheery group.

He would go check in on his mother, though he planned not to mention his new winnings at the table, and then make arrangements to travel down to visit the Standish sisters. God willing, he could establish good solutions for their situation and living and have them well in hand within a few weeks.

Chapter Two

Miss June Standish ran her finger down the ledger, calculating expenses, the infernal drafts in the cottage sending a trail of gooseflesh up her arms. She pulled her thickest shawl tighter around her shoulders. The hour was early yet. None of her sisters had ventured downstairs, but their remaining in bed might have more to do with the chill in the air than them being asleep. Though she assumed her youngest sister, Grace, continued to sleep soundly.

They could probably burn more wood. They had a budget for it. Ever since the Duke of Granbury inherited their cottage and castle, things had improved. But they didn't have enough servants to get the fire going in the morning. And the way she looked at it, once you left your bed, you may as well venture downstairs to be in the kitchen where it was warmest anyway. Perhaps they should hire another servant.

The castle renovations were under way. She wasn't certain she wanted to move with her sisters into another infernally drafty place, but His Grace had assured her the living areas of the castle would be superior to her current situation. They were scheduled to move in next month.

He had also assured her that her chances of marrying would

improve if they lived in the castle. Anyone who didn't know their royal connections would be made aware, simply by their inhabiting the old seat.

She sighed. If only she could see each of her sisters happily married.

Grace stepped into the kitchen, her blankets wrapped around her.

June stood. "Grace, what are you doing up so early?"

"I couldn't sleep. This house makes noises."

"We've been here long enough for you to know the noises don't mean a thing."

"They have to mean something. I was more worried about them when we first arrived, but I'll admit, sometimes I see an old, weathered sailor with absurdly long fingernails scratching on my window."

"Goodness. You do have an imagination."

Grace shrugged and sat as close to June as she could. "What are you working on?"

"I'm determining if we need another servant."

"A lady's maid?"

June laughed. "And what do we need one of those for?"

"To do our hair, help us dress..."

"We have each other."

"But a maid could do the modern styles, help us look our very best. His Grace said we'd be having a Season."

"The others will. You are still too young to be out."

She groaned in frustration. "Really, am I too young for everything?"

"No, you are just the right age to help me get some water boiling."

"A cook. We should hire another assistant for cook."

June had thought of it. "I think the castle has its own staff as well, so when we blend there, we can work out different responsibilities among the staff. It's just one more month."

Grace grinned. "I can't wait. I love the castle. And then no one can forbid me to enter or explore, because we will all live there."

"That is true. There will be areas blocked off for safety reasons while the renovations continue, but we shall have a rather large area that is our own living space."

"Do you think this is what Uncle wanted for us?"

"Perhaps." June toyed with her quill. They had all loved their uncle, the Earl of Beaufort, as old and confused as he sometimes became. He had swept in and picked up the pieces of their broken lives, hugged the loneliness out of them, and helped them feel centered and loved. His loss was one of their greatest, almost to the intensity of losing their parents. "Regardless of his intent, we are making the best of it, are we not?"

"Yes. I'm just grateful we have each other." She curled closer and rested her head on June's shoulder.

"I feel the same, sweet." She tipped her head so it rested on the top of Grace's. They sat thus for a moment more. Then June knew it was time to begin the day. "We have our studies this morning. And our dancing instruction this afternoon."

"Will we ever have a man to practice with?"

"Someday, when we dance the real thing." June laughed. "Am I not a good enough dance partner?"

"You're excellent." Grace's tone and expression said just the opposite.

"I hope one day to see you all happily wed. You know that. Perhaps with the duke's help, we can secure good matches for each one of you."

"And you." Grace's large and caring eyes made June's heart clench.

"You are a dear, but I might feel happiest just to see each one of you settled."

"And perhaps one of us will marry gobs of money, enough to care for us until our dying days."

"That would be wonderful, but the only thing I ask is you also marry for happiness."

Grace nodded. "But don't you think all manner of happiness could be found, if the living is comfortable?"

"I suppose." June didn't wish to fill her sister's head with romantic fancies. For a woman in the Standish sisters' financial state could not afford to be romantic in her choice of marriage partner. But they could insist on happiness, on comfort or security. She hoped they could at least strive for that.

After a modest breakfast, all five sisters met in the music and school room. June smiled at them all. Every now and then, she had to relax about their many worries and just appreciate the good that surrounded them. Grace, Lucy, Kate, and Charity were the best of women, the very best she knew, at any rate, and she was intensely proud of every one.

They'd converted an additional sitting room to their place of projects. On one end, the easels were set, with large, billowing fabric covering the floor to catch the paint. They had a pianoforte, a smaller harp, needlepoint, and on the other end of the room, a large blackboard and a bookshelf full of books. Their library might be small compared to some, but it was full of June's most prized possessions.

As the only Standish daughter who'd had a governess, and she for only a short amount of time, June spent an hour every day working on their deportment, the rules of society, their manners, and their general instruction in the ways of a gently bred lady.

"And what if I do not wish for a gently bred man?" Charity's stubborn streak grew the longer they lived in Sussex. June wasn't sure what drove her stronger sensibilities.

"I just want you happy, and in most cases, that means with enough food on the table, an established place to live, and a good man. If that can be found in the working classes, then all the happier I will be, since you profess to prefer such a life."

"'Such a life.' What a snob you are, June."

"Tsk. She's not a snob." Kate shifted her skirts. "She does well by us to show us how to present ourselves. I, for one, do not wish to be embarrassed when next the Duchess of York stops in."

"Oh, she is the utmost. That woman's nose is so far in the air, I'm surprised she can walk." Charity shook her head.

"We are grateful for their goodness to us. All our fine dresses come from her and the others."

"Yes." Kate slumped in her seat. "Last year's fashions."

"And still plenty ostentatious." Charity lifted her skirts. "Who needs embroidery on the hem? Lace I can see, but embroidery? It just gets dirty on these roads and is impossible to wash out."

"Then don't be wearing the embroidery while out exploring the dirty roads." Kate poked her needle into the handkerchief she was sewing.

"What are you making?" June leaned closer.

"I'm hoping to have a stack of these for when we go to dinners and balls in Brighton. Then a man could know where to return it." She'd sewn pretty flowers on the edges, as well as her initials and Northumber Castle.

"That's lovely." June lifted her book. "Now, allow me to finish." She read to them from Shakespeare, and had more interest than in her previous descriptions of the early royal lineage. They would follow up the literature lesson with French, and then lunch.

In a break in her reading, Grace piped up, "We'll have dancing this afternoon."

"Do we have Jacques to come instruct us?" Charity's hopeful expression gave June pause.

"No, not today. We will be working on the country dances. And those are simple enough to memorize without Jacques. He will come next week for the waltz."

"Oh, I love the waltz." Grace clapped her hands together.

"As do I." Kate put down her embroidery, her black, shiny curls bouncing at her neck. "Do you think we could have a new bonnet for the promenade on Tuesday?"

"What promenade?" June searched her memory for mention of a promenade.

"Oh, come, June. Pay attention. Prinny will be back in town, and everyone will begin walking up and down the green. Everyone who is here will attend. It is the prime location for us to be seen and make an impression." She paused in a rather dramatic manner. "*If* we make a good impression."

"I wish to make a good impression. Do you think we need new bonnets?" Grace looked from June to Kate and back.

"I think we will make the best impression, no matter what kind of bonnets are on our heads." June set the book aside. But inside she worried about just such a thing. Would they be able to be seen as anything other than charity to the gentry? Perhaps a bonnet would help? She shook her head. Everything seemed so overwhelming at times. She'd never had a Season herself. Her parents had fallen ill, and were taken from them around the time she would have started to prepare. What did she really know about any such thing? "No matter what, we must be a Standish daughter, women with a heritage to be proud of."

Stenson stepped into their small parlor. "The Duchess of Sussex here to see you."

June sucked in her breath. The arrival of the Duchess was a mixed blessing. "You know how we must receive her."

They all stood taller, painted blank expressions on their faces, and moved to the front sitting room, reserved almost solely for visits from the nobility—and in this case, the royal family. As soon as they were situated, each with a different manner of amusement—embroidery, reading, drawing, and two opposite a chess board, though no one had moved a single piece in ages—Stenson opened their door. "The Duchess of Sussex."

The Standish sisters stood and curtsied.

Their guest smiled, and her eyes twinkled. "Oh, my lovelies, my dears. Let me have a look at you." She held out her hands. She kept such a youth and vigor about her, June had vowed to do the same. Kate admired her clothing. Lucy coveted her title, and Charity looked at her with great suspicion.

June curtseyed again. "It is good to see you, Your Grace. You do us honor by your visit."

"I find so much happiness aiding in your situation, such as it is." She studied them for a moment, and June wondered if she'd break out in tears right then. "Oh, and aren't you the most deserving." She placed hands on her heart. "To think, so reduced in situation, so noble in bearing. You are all to be commended for your fortitude."

"Thank you, Your Grace." June dipped her head. "Would you care for some tea? Coffee?"

"Oh, thank you, if you can spare some."

"We have ample." June nodded to their maid, who waited just outside the door.

As soon as Her Grace was seated, she adjusted her skirts. They flowed in an elegant manner to the floor. The delicate flowers that lined her hemline, the tiny sparkles of gems which glittered when the sun touched them, must have been fascinating to June's most fashion-conscious sister, Kate.

"Has the Duchess of York been by?" The Duchess of Sussex asked, as though she didn't care, but June knew their answer would pester and bother her for days.

And Charity did too. "She has, and she brought us the most exquisite gowns. They must have been her own, they were so lovely. To everyone who asks, we must positively gush about the Duchess of York and her deep generosity."

"Oh, did she? That's nice, isn't it? Hmm." She narrowed her eyes and waved her hand. A servant in the Sussex livery appeared in the doorway as if summoned from invisibility. "Please bring in the packages."

He nodded.

"Well, I have brought some of my own."

Kate gasped and placed hands at the side of her face. "Oh, thank you, Your Grace, for your sense of style is exquisite. I have been studying just now how perfectly you wear your clothing. Of all the ladies, you are my most favorite."

The duchess beamed. "I appreciate a woman who understands the finer details of fashion. Which one are you?" She lifted a quizzing glass. "Come here."

Kate almost tripped over herself to rush to Her Grace's side.

"Ah, yes. Miss Kate, is it?"

"Yes, Your Grace. If it pleases you."

"You shall have my brooch."

Their sister Lucy gasped, but June waved her to hush.

"Thank you." Kate's curtsy was low and grateful.

"I have brought dishes as well, and some food from cook's kitchen. We live near enough you should be recipients of our finest."

"Thank you. You could not dote upon more grateful servants."

"Now that we are here in Brighton for a smaller Season, I plan to visit often. Whenever we are in our Sussex estate, we will be sure to pay you a call."

"We will look forward to the honor."

The tea service arrived. "How would you like your tea?"

They ate and sipped, and the duchess filled them in on the gossip of the *ton* and from London.

"Oh, you sisters would love London. Imagine a Season in Town. Wouldn't that be so exciting! I cannot fathom how your forbearers could leave you with so little, so paltry your opportunities to attend such delights as a Season. I know a handsome earl. He would be perfect for one of you." She clucked. "A pity you could not go even one Season."

"Yes, pity." Charity's look of mock sorrow almost made June laugh, and she hoped the duchess would not see the duplicitous expression. Did the duchess not know the hurt her words could cause? Or did she really think the sisters didn't feel their situation keenly enough without her comments?

They chatted a few moments more and then bade the woman

goodbye. She left piles of things in the entry. June should be grateful for the gifts, and she was. But unless the gowns fit, it was an expense to alter them, or a lot of work for the sisters. Kate was becoming quite proficient with a needle.

After lunch, and once the duchess departed, the sisters gathered back in the music room. Grace sat at the piano. "But I wish to dance this time. Someone give me a chance to practice the steps."

"We will, but after the rest of us have a go. You're the youngest."

"I know." Grace frowned. "So you all keep saying."

"Well, there is less a need for you to learn, as you won't even be dancing."

"Thank you, Lucy."

"We all know Lucy is going to marry money, and then the rest of us won't have to worry about getting married." Charity waved her hand in Lucy's direction.

"I'd like to get married." Kate pouted. "And so would everyone else, I imagine, including June."

"Yes, even me. But we'll worry about the rest of you first." She hid her sadness. *Even June.* She was not a spinster, not even close to being on the shelf, but she just didn't think she could spend the effort getting herself married when she had so many others to be concerned with.

Grace started in on a well-known country dance, and June called out the steps while she did them. "You see? I start, and then I must add my own flair here. You watch and repeat."

The girls stepped together with imaginary partners, waited while their partners would have done the same, and then repeated. It was a bit confusing at times, but it worked well enough.

Then Stenson, their very young butler, stepped into the room. "A Lord Morley to see you."

The girls froze. Kate whispered, "Who?"

June's heart skipped, and the pause between beats thundered

in her chest. "I—" Her voice cracked. "I do believe that is Morley?"

"The nice man who came with the duke? He's an earl?"

"Yes, he was introduced as such, but His Grace called him Morley so often, the 'earl' part didn't stick. I do hope we did not follow suit and omit his title." Lucy clucked. "To neglect to use a man's title without permission is an insult in the highest order."

"Yes, thank you, Lucy." June stood and straightened her dress, urging the girls to rise as well. They rolled the carpet back where it should be and patted down their hair. "Send him in, Stenson."

He nodded. "Very good, miss."

"Does anyone else think Stenson looks like a young boy playing a part?" Charity giggled.

"Hush." June shook her head.

And in walked Lord Morley, the man she'd thought of constantly since their meeting, the most handsome man of her albeit limited acquaintance. He filled the room with his large stature, his strong shoulders, his brilliant jawline, with the crisp white of his cravat brushing against it. His gaze flitted through the sisters and rested on June. And then the corner of his mouth lifted in a soft smile. "Miss Standish." He bowed. "Miss Charity, Miss Lucy, Miss Kate, and Miss Grace."

Grace giggled from behind the piano.

They all curtsied.

Then June stepped forward. "We are so happy you have come. Please, take a seat. Would you like some tea?"

"Tea would be wonderful, thank you."

Grace tripped off to the kitchen to inform their cook.

And June wasn't sure she could form words. Why had he come? The idea he would arrive to pay a social call filled her with hope, a hope she tried to tamp out.

"Tell us the news of London." Kate asked all their visitors to talk of London. Usually she was most seeking news of fashion, but as Lord Morley would likely know little of those kinds of details, June supposed Kate would be satisfied with whatever snippets she could glean.

"Things are warming up in London, just enough to almost be pleasant." He laughed. "Not many families stayed on. I expect the Season to pick up in high form in a month or two. I hear many of the families have come to Brighton."

"We hear the same." Kate fluffed her skirts. "In fact, we were just talking of doing a promenade on the green tomorrow. Will you be staying long?"

"I will be here for a few weeks or more, I believe." His gaze flitted to June's.

June didn't respond, for she wasn't sure what to say at all to his statement. She was most desperately pleased, but so impatient with herself for thinking in such a way. Charity kicked her ankle. June started. "I'm happy to hear it. Would you care to join us tomorrow in our promenade? Like Miss Kate said, you are likely to see most everyone from Brighton at one point or another on the green."

"I should very much enjoy the outing, thank you."

The tea arrived, and June busied herself with the pouring. Why had he come? She couldn't account for it. And even though his gaze rested on her more than anywhere else, nothing could make sense in her mind as to why that would be.

Chapter Three

Morley sipped his tea. "You have a lovely room here. What was I interrupting? From the looks of it, great reading, studies, and perhaps some music?"

"Yes, we were dancing. June teaches us when the instructor cannot come. It's not as lovely as if we had partners, but it is fun, even though I'm on the pianoforte." Grace, the youngest, talked a great deal.

Morley enjoyed her the last time he had come. "And have you had opportunity to explore the castle, as you most desired?"

"We have not." June seemed to find the crumbling state of the building depressing.

Grace smiled and leaned forward in her seat. "Will you be doing any exploring of the castle while you are here?"

"Grace." June's smile warmed Morley's heart.

"I would indeed like to do some exploring, and I welcome all Standish sisters who care to come."

"Oh, I would love to come." Grace clasped her hands. "It is absolutely my fondest desire to visit the castle."

"Then you shall come, if your sister will allow?"

They both turned to Miss Standish. Grace gave such an expression of pleading, Morley wasn't sure how anyone resisted the girl. And Miss Standish smiled, which brought the sun into the room.

"Will all of you join me?" His eyes met Miss Standish's again, and he saw her reluctance. He dipped his head. "Or if you'd rather, I can explore on my own. I must check on the state of things, the progress in the construction."

June cleared her throat. "We would be happy to come. Thank you for the invitation. I don't wish to overwhelm. In the spare five minutes since you've arrived, we are promenading and visiting the castle together. Surely you have more to do than entertain the Standish sisters."

Ah, so perhaps he was overstepping. "I understand. I shall not trespass upon your kindness much more than is necessary."

Kate shook her head. "You are not trespassing at all. In fact, I have another invitation still. If you will be here for a few weeks, then you must attend the assembly. There are dances and a good selection of people. Perhaps you'd enjoy it?" Kate was the strong beauty of the sisters. And she held herself differently, as though she already knew she was meant for the nobility.

"And you have intrigued me with yet another opportunity here in Brighton. I thank you for helping me feel so immediately integrated into the neighborhood."

"Our pleasure." Kate sipped her tea.

After several breaths of silence, with Morley wondering just how much Miss Standish wanted his company, he nodded to Charity. "And what are you working on there?"

She started, her quill flying across the page, but she didn't look up until she'd used up her ink. Dipping in her inkwell, she looked up. "Oh. Well, I..."

"Charity writes stories. She's deep into the middle of a tragic gothic romance." Grace grinned.

"Are you now?" Morley was intrigued. "And do you ever share your stories?"

"She does. But just to us." Grace hurried across the room and sat back down at the piano. "Would you like to help us practice our country dances?" She played the opening bar of a light, energetic song he recognized. "They will be doing these very ones at the assembly."

"Oh, then I should very much like a refresher on the steps, so that I might not scuff up some lovely lady's slippers."

"Grace. We needn't trouble His Lordship with a request such as yours." The look June gave Grace should have squelched her desires. But instead her bottom lip stuck out.

"He said he'd like to."

June's gaze searched his own.

He smiled. "I would enjoy a country dance. Anything we can do to help all you lovely ladies make the best impression."

Miss Standish gave him a strange look and then nodded slowly. "Very well, then. Let's just do the shortest of the bunch we know."

Kate joined her. "It's the one most often played at the assemblies anyway."

Morley bowed in front of Miss Standish. "Would you do me the honor?"

"Me?" She looked away and then back. "Um, yes. I would." She curtsied, and then they stood across from each other in the space allowed in the center of the room. The others joined their square, and the dance began. Miss Standish led out, so he had to watch carefully, but he found her steps easy to follow and her dancing delightful. Whenever their eyes met, she smiled. He couldn't tell if his presence was enjoyed or endured, but he found her attention pleasant and that of her sisters delightful. And for the first time, he didn't curse Gerald for his conniving.

He circled with Miss Standish and then took Kate around and then back to Miss Standish. They laughed and made merry. When the playing finished, he bowed before them all. "I haven't had so much fun in a country dance in ages. Thank you."

"And now we shall be prepared at the assembly."

"Precisely. I thank you again." He bowed. "And now, how are

the plans going for the move to the castle? What can we do to help?"

He sat on the same sofa Miss Standish had occupied, but then she took another. For the first time, Lucy joined more of the conversation. "We have every room planned out. Crates will arrive, and the servants shall pack them up. We can assist, naturally, but it isn't right if we are seen hauling our things..."

"Oh, not to worry. You certainly can rely on me and the servants to get you moved properly."

"You?"

"Well, certainly. And I do feel you will be needing an increase in footmen. The castle has its own, but even with the addition of the staff already there, I feel it prudent to hire on some extras."

"Oh, that's lovely. Shall they have our own livery?"

"Yes. I've looked into it, actually. Northumber Castle, and indeed your Standish family name, has a renowned and respected coat of arms and livery. So measures need to be taken for those uniforms." He paused. The ladies were silent. "Assuming you are in agreement?" he said.

"Certainly we are. Is that not right, June?" Kate rested a hand on Miss Standish's arm.

"I have no complaints."

Kate nudged her again.

"Oh, I'm terribly sorry. And thank you. This is all too kind and much more than any of us expected."

"I'm happy to be of assistance."

He stayed for another hour, enjoying their company. Kate read to him from their poetry assignments. And then he shocked Miss Standish by sharing a poem by Byron. Grace played more on the pianoforte and sang, which he found lovely.

At length, and with some regret, he stood. "Thank you for the lovely visit. I've been charmed in every way."

"Oh, no. You cannot leave without hearing June on the harp. She sings the loveliest French piece." Kate held a hand to her heart. "I imagine men would swoon just at the hearing of her beautiful voice."

"Kate!" June's face turned the brightest of reds, and she shook her head. "Lord Morley has heard quite enough of the Standish sisters today. I imagine he's had enough to last a month, at least." She stood at his side. "I'll walk you out."

He chuckled but dipped his head. "Thank you for the attention. I would enjoy hearing you sing though, especially after such high praise."

"Oh, stop, please. She doesn't know."

"I do, too," said Kate. "And you're an angel."

June waved her sister away and hurried him from the room. "Thank you for stopping by. I cannot account for the distinction of a visit, but we are grateful, nonetheless. You helped pass what might have been a rather dull afternoon."

"I am pleased to have been a part. I look forward to our promenade."

Stenson held open the door, and Miss Standish stood just inside as Morley stepped into his carriage. "We shall talk more of your move at the promenade. Until then, *au revoir*."

"*Au revoir*." Miss Standish stood and waved until he could no longer see her.

Once his carriage had rounded the bend, he sat back in on his bench and closed his eyes. Charming family. Even Miss Charity, who had been quiet most of the afternoon, scribbling on her sheaves of paper, had been lovely. And Miss Standish was the most lovely of all.

The eldest, an engaging, honestly fascinating woman, who obviously had no interest in him whatsoever, would have less so when she learned he was, in fact, the owner of the estate. But perhaps he could keep the knowledge from her as long as possible, at least until he knew her better.

They drove along through town. What a lovely little location just outside of Brighton. When the coachman pulled into his inn, he was ready to write some correspondence and rest for the evening.

But upon entering the front door, a ruckus greeted his ears, and a familiar voice called his name.

"Lord Morley! Morley, my friend! Join us." A tall man with dark, curly hair—and a boyish grin that convinced all the ladies he was charming—waved to Morley.

A group of his peers from the House of Lords and from London in general sat at a table, mildly into their cups already.

He approached, pleased to see them. "What are you lot doing here?"

"Everyone's here. London is dull as ever." Lord Weatherby lifted up his cup and then downed half of it in one swallow. "We'll be promenading tomorrow, and Kenworthy has set up cards at his place every night, if you're looking." Lord Weatherby's smile grew. "It'll be our own gaming establishment."

A lazy, light-haired cad, who Morley barely countenanced, lifted his many-ringed finger. "Do join us. I'd like someone else there with a bit more purse, if you know what I mean."

"Just because some of us are still on our father's allowance." Arrington waved to the server. "If I keep winning like I have, you're going to be the one low on blunt."

Lord Smallwood flicked something off his jacket. "That's not likely to happen, is it?" His gaze lifted to Morley again. "Join us. What brings you to Brighton?"

Morley pulled up a chair, and the server brought him a cup full of ale without him asking. His gaze surveyed his peers. "Kenworthy, Weatherby, Arrington, Smallwood,...this group spells trouble if I ever saw one."

They lifted their cups and clinked together in the middle. "Join us. You haven't always been so staid." Weatherby grinned.

"I haven't always been the Earl of Morley either."

"Tosh." Smallwood shrugged. "Don't see how that has to change anything."

The men watched him, and Morley suddenly felt the need to

keep his business closer to his chest. "I'm here though, aren't I? Time to leave London for the beauties of Brighton."

"The beauties? Is the confirmed bachelorhood of Lord Morley about to be challenged by a bit of a skirt?" Weatherby's smug expression made Morley want to discuss anything else somewhere else. But he kept his seat. "I was referring to the sea. But I'm not opposed to a pretty face."

"Ho ho!" Kenworthy grinned. "Who would be?" They all lifted their cups again.

"I'm here to aid the Standish sisters, actually."

Conversation stopped, and Lord Smallwood's smile grew in a slow, snakelike fashion. "Are you, now? And in what manner are you giving them aid?"

"That will be none of your business." He toyed with his glass. "But now seems a good time to mention they're looking for respectability, and those are the kinds of offers I'll be considering."

"Taking offers for them? Are you some sort of guardian?"

He sighed. "His Grace passed them off."

"I heard it differently. I heard you won the castle, the cottage, and a whole lot of coin in a card game last month." Weatherby's eyes gleamed. "Will they be getting dowries?"

"His Grace arranged modest ones. But they're lovely and deserve a good match, so if that's not you, spread the word."

The men quieted for a moment. Perhaps the mention of serious marriage opportunities sobered them all. Perhaps they were uninterested, which would suit Morley just fine. He hoped their loose speech would help get the word out, and the right sort of men would see the good in the Standish sisters. He wanted to do well by them. They deserved a secure and happy life.

He wanted to curse Gerald's name again. Instead, he closed his lips and said nothing more on the topic.

Chapter Four

T he house was full of happy chatter. June finished the last touches on her hair. She slept in the master bedroom, the one meant for her parents, were they still alive. And even though it was the largest room and a part of her thought the sisters who shared a room—Kate and Lucy— might benefit from the space, she couldn't give it up. The solitude gave her enough strength to face the noise and stress of everyday life.

Shouts from the other end of the cottage made her smile. "Charity! May I borrow your slippers?"

"What will I wear?"

"Your other slippers."

"No."

"Please! I cannot bear to wear these old, faded things."

"No one sees them. They're fully under your skirts."

"Just wear mine. I can't stand your begging." Lucy's impatience was her greatest vice but sometimes her strongest asset.

June smiled. She loved these sisters of hers. Her gaze lifted to the portrait of her parents on the wall. As she stared into the painted eyes of her mother, she whispered, "How am I doing, Mama?"

With no answer to the question any time she asked, she stood and kept moving forward, for what else could she do but her best and hope everything worked out?

When she left her room and stood at the top of her stairs, she held her head high. She liked this particular hairstyle, and her dress flattered her. Even if their efforts to find good matches for her sisters were not directed at her in any way, she would represent the Standish sisters well.

The last time the Duchess of York visited, she had been so kind. Just about every member of the peerage who visited suggested who they should try to marry. The Duchess was no exception. June knew it was kindly meant, but no more was ever done to help the suggestion come to fruition, until the Duke of Granbury. She smiled. He was a good man. She'd heard he married his second love, Amelia. He deserved such a happy event in his life.

"Are we ready?" she called quietly down the upstairs hallway.

Charity came first. She wore a beautiful, deep blue. It brought out the striking color of her eyes. Her hair was tied back in a simple knot, but her face was clean and her gloves as well which might be all the effort Charity wished to exert at the moment.

"You look lovely."

"Thank you. I don't have much of a desire to meet anyone on this outing. I'm looking forward more to seeing the promenade itself. What do people do? Simply walk about on the lawn? I'm so intrigued."

"I don't know either. If it's anything at all like Hyde Park, that's exactly what they do."

Lucy joined them. "And, of course, we must behave with the utmost decorum. We are outside on a beautiful day in the park, Charity, but this does not mean the situation calls for romps and rolling about on hills, or laughing over loud, or—"

"I think she understands." June smiled at Lucy, who looked unconvinced.

Kate joined them next with an overabundance of extra ribbons. On anyone else, the look might have seemed overdone, but on Kate, it just made her all the more charming. Her bonnet covered just enough of her face, and the lovely purple tied under her chin brought out her own complexion.

"I don't know why you should get all the extra ribbons." Lucy sniffed.

"Because no one else wanted them. Just because now you can see what I've done doesn't mean they should have been yours to begin with." She lifted her chin. "A little creativity can do beautiful things to our limited wardrobes."

Grace at last joined them, and June smiled at her youngest sister. She'd dressed like the others, but there was an air of youth about her, a sense of someone still in the schoolroom, and June was grateful for at least that.

As they made their way down the stairs, Kate sighed.

"What?"

"I wish, just once, there would be a whole mass of handsome men at the bottom of these stairs, looking up at us, ready to take our hands." Kate rested her hand on the railing. "But I shall not be melancholy. We are going to promenade. We're going to assemblies. It feels like a bit of a fairy tale. There was a time, I thought we'd be locked up in our tiny cottage forever."

"Isn't the Duke of Granbury wonderful?" Grace skipped to the bottom of the stairs.

And then a knock sounded on the door.

"Who could it be?"

Grace almost opened it, but June called out, "Stenson will take care of that."

"Oh, true." Grace stepped to the side and allowed their butler room to open the door.

Lord Morley entered with a flourish, dressed in top hat, cane, and jacket, his breeches fitting splendidly, his grin wide, and his bow deep.

Behind him, a magnificent carriage waited in front of their cottage.

"We don't have to walk!" Grace jumped up and down.

And Lord Morley laughed. "You most certainly do not. I have come to fetch the loveliest ladies in all of Brighton for a promenade." He held out his elbows, and Lucy and Kate each grabbed one. A quick wink over his shoulder sent June's stomach leaping around, tickling her insides.

Charity linked her arm. "He's everything a man should be, June."

Surprised, she turned to her usually unromantic sister. "Do you think so?"

"I do, and I think you should let him know as much."

"What!" June looked away, her face warming.

"There's no reason you can't marry like the rest of us."

"And you? Are you going to marry?"

"I might." The secretive smile on Charity's face rose some suspicion in June's mind, but she decided to press her sister more on the topic later.

Lord Morley had assisted her other three sisters into the carriage already. Charity stepped forward. He helped her alight, and then he turned to June.

His gaze intensified as he held a hand out to her. "Miss Standish, your carriage."

She dipped her head. "You are too kind." When her fingers rested on his palm, a lovely feeling of warmth spread through her. Not the tingly kind of response she'd often read about when two people fell in love, but the reassuring, trusting kind. When their eyes connected again, she smiled, thinking she might prefer this warmth to any other.

She found a seat in the overly populated carriage and was surprised when Lord Morley closed the door without entering.

"And where will you sit?" Grace leaned forward.

"I shall ride up top with the coachman. Perhaps he will let me direct the horses."

"And that's what I think would be the most diverting." Charity lifted her chin.

Lord Morley seemed greatly amused by her observation. "Perhaps I can return with a smaller cart, and you could help direct the horse that would lead the more manageable conveyance?"

Charity's smile, so seldomly gifted, filled her face. "I should like it very much."

"Then we shall make it happen."

He bowed to them all. They felt the motion as he climbed aboard, and then the equipage began to move.

"I hope we meet many new people." Kate, who sat closest to the window, peered outside. "Didn't someone say Brighton is full of people visiting from London?

"Yes. I believe we might have an opportunity to make new acquaintances. Lord Morley might know some we don't." June couldn't help her smile as she thought of him.

"Why is he being so kind to us?" Grace tapped her toes.

"He is a kind man," Lucy asserted.

But Charity laughed. "No man, as kind as he may be, would suddenly care for a bunch of almost-spinster sisters out of the goodness of his heart. Can you not guess why he is paying us attention?" She turned her gaze to June.

"We do not know such a thing. It would be unwise to speculate or to create expectations." June shook her head, but could do nothing to control the increased beating of her heart.

"And yet I can think of no other reason. What will you say if he asks to call?"

"Why must he ask? He already comes to call." Grace frowned.

"Not just to call, Grace—to *call*."

"Oh." She studied them, apparently deep in thought. "*Oh*." Then she smiled. "Will he? Ask to call?"

"If he asks in that way, I would, of course, encourage him, but I shan't do any encouraging at all until he asks. I don't want to seem the desperate, clamoring sort." June turned to each of her sisters. "And neither should any of you. Just because we don't have as many resources as others does not mean we are without friends. Even though I would love more than anything to see each of you happily situated, I do not feel it should arrive as a result of conniving tricks and trappings."

"I don't even know what all those things are." Kate shrugged. "I say we just go for a walk on the green. Isn't that what a promenade is?"

"You are absolutely right." June lifted the cover to peek out the window. "Would you look."

They passed the huge palace Prince George was building. Big, pointing spindles on top of round and bulbous rooftops filled the sky to their right.

"The palace is the most remarkable thing I've ever seen." Kate looked as though every fashionable dream of her heart were being fulfilled in that moment.

"I can't believe we haven't come to see it yet." Lucy's eyes were just as wide and staring.

"It is a rather long walk." Charity as usual seemed nonplussed.

"I suppose. Another reason to be grateful for Lord Morley and his carriage." Grace smiled.

The carriage slowed to a stop, and Lord Morley stood again at the door. "We have arrived." He bowed. "And who is ready for a lovely promenade?"

"I am quite ready," Grace called from inside the carriage.

As soon as they were out on the lawn, the warm sun shining on a chilly, otherwise-brisk day, June was even more happy they'd come. The sun filled her with hope and happiness, and all her worries seemed to carry away on the breeze.

Lord Morley lowered his voice and leaned closer to them, so they moved in to hear. His face was close to June's, so close she felt the puffs of his breath on the top of her head.

"I shall introduce you to as many as I dare. There will be some I'd rather you not know, and others I would most particularly like you to meet. How about we have a meeting afterward and discuss which types are which?" His grin was small, conspiratorial.

"I would be most grateful for all insight you have, Lord Morley." June placed a hand on his arm.

"Then I shall invite myself to your home when we are finished here, and we shall discuss all the happenings of today." He placed his hand over June's, which still rested on his arm. "Shall we?"

She stood at his side. "Yes, let's."

They walked together, away from the carriage, to a great green field of sorts where people simply walked along. Small groups talked with one another, and many strolled together. Paired-off couples were not so much the norm, as clusters and larger circles of flowing skirts and straight jackets. The Season had not yet begun, and no alliances had been formed—or at least that's how it looked to June.

"So many people are here."

"Yes, I came across some of my peers last night. They said even more are arriving. In many ways, it is fantastic news for you and your sisters."

For her? She searched his face. He didn't seem to mean anything particular by his comment, but to June, it suggested he was not interested in pursuing anything with her, like her sisters suspected. She almost removed her hand from his arm, but then thought better of it. He was being incredibly dear to her family, and she could be a friend in return. But the disappointment hurt a little.

They approached a waiting group of men.

"Ooh." Kate smiled.

Each one more handsome than the next, they carried themselves like men of title. June assumed they were not to be hoped for.

But when they saw Lord Morley and her sisters, each one stood taller and immediately made their way over.

Lord Morley stiffened. "Here we go."

"What? Are they not to be trusted?"

"Out here on the green? They are harmless." He lifted a hand in greeting.

When they were close enough, he introduced each one of June's sisters to Lords Kenworthy, Weatherby, Arrington, and Smallwood, the last of which paid June particular attention, his eyes drinking in hers in a manner she'd never seen before.

When each of her sisters had paired with another, Grace latching on to Lord Morley, Lord Smallwood held out his arm for her. "I would be honored if I could accompany you, Miss Standish."

"Thank you."

His arm was strong, his carriage confident. When he smiled down into her face, she felt dazzled by his teeth, his eyes, his handsome attention. Her gaze flitted to Lord Morley's, and his disapproving darkness dimmed her happiness, but then Lord Smallwood started walking with her at his side. "Come, we shall get to know each other. This fine day is one for dreaming, is it not?"

What a pleasant diversion. No harm could come from entertaining many, becoming acquainted with the men of the peerage. Her attention would be spared for no other, at least for the moment.

Chapter Five

M orley bristled and growled inside, surging with concern the longer Smallwood and Miss Standish walked together. Their heads were bent just the tiniest amount toward one another, and now and then, a delicious laugh carried over the breeze from their direction.

But Grace carried on beside him with all the happiest tidbits and tellings from their family life. Soon he was more focused on her and her stories of June Standish than on the real person who walked with one of the greatest cads in all of England, with June apparently enthralled by his nonsense.

"Did you know she loves bridges? And small streams. And trees. She loves when the leaves bud and the flowers begin to show. I think spring is her favorite season. One time she had us plant bulbs in the fall. She gave me this ugly, round, dirty thing and told me to place it in the earth. When winter ended and the days turned warmer, she was out there every day, checking the soil, waiting for the green tips to show." Grace laughed, her eyes shining. "You have never seen a more joyful June than the day she came running to show us that the bulbs had started to come up."

Morley laughed and was all the more enchanted.

They approached a larger group, where a chattering energy filled the air, and he welcomed the opportunity to broaden the Standish sisters' acquaintance. They needed some feminine influence.

But he needn't have worried.

The sisters were soon swarmed by women, interested in their welfare, happy they had made an appearance on the lawn, making eyes at the lords who accompanied them. Lord Morley didn't know half of this group of ladies, but the Standishes seemed acquainted with them. He stepped back, away from many hopeful eyes blinking up at him.

The air had heated, and they had been walking for longer than Lord Morley planned. Grace's face looked flushed. He led her away. "Are you well?"

"I think so, but a drink of something would be nice."

"Perhaps we should make our way back?"

She nodded, and he suggested they turn the other direction, at least to make headway toward the carriage.

Smallwood still captured Miss Standish's hand on his arm, and her attention. She hadn't once looked in his direction.

As he made his way to the carriage, Charity joined him on his other arm. He smiled at her. "And what has happened to Weatherby?"

"I sent him away."

Morley laughed. "You did what?"

"I did. I sent him away."

"How does one send away a viscount?"

"Well, he wanted to talk about the weather first, then the Season, and the prettiness of my skin, and I got bored. So I started talking about Wellington and the war and the brilliance in a mathematical equation."

Morley chuckled. "And he went running?"

"Exactly."

He encouraged her to place her hand on his other arm. "While I'm highly amused, it is only because we are talking about Weatherby. He's not one I've taken seriously in many years. But what if he was a respectable, decent Lord who would make you a fine match?"

"If he is not able to stomach my talking of math in his presence, then we might not be the best match after all."

Morley didn't know what to say in response. "Perhaps you can save those conversations for a time when you know each other better?"

"Perhaps." Charity pressed her lips together.

Morley suspected there was more to say—much more—but he didn't pester it out of her.

Smallwood took a ridiculously long amount of time to say goodbye to Miss Standish, and then they were all once again back in his carriage. Smallwood called up to him in the coachman's chair, "Taking an unexpected interest in this family, aren't you?"

"Not unexpected, no." He nodded to his coachman. "Take us home, Charles."

"Yes, my lord." The coachman commanded the horses, and they were off.

WHEN THEY WERE ALL SITTING COMFORTABLY IN THE SITTING room at the sisters' cottage, Morley had to chuckle to himself while watching them. They talked of this person or that. The energy was high, and soon the slippers were off and little stockinged feet peeked out beneath skirts. And for a moment, he felt as though he'd entered a large family.

Miss Standish ordered tea and sandwiches and lemonade. "I'm so thirsty." She fanned herself. When her eyes fell on him, they widened a moment, and then she laughed. "Sisters, we have forgotten dear Morley—that is to say, *Lord* Morley—is here with us."

"I didn't forget." Grace had come to sit beside him and had

quickly become lost in a book. "He just fits so comfortably that not much more needs to be done about the fact."

Morley smiled. "I am grateful to be a part and to comfortably abide here with you, but I would like to address a couple things about this afternoon."

They turned eyes to him.

"First off, what did you think?"

"I loved it." Kate clapped her hands together. "Lord Kenworthy was attentive and in every way a gentleman. Do you approve of him, Lord Morley?"

"I do. Of all the men in the group we met, he is the one I can say without hesitation I approve of."

"The only one?" Miss Standish's eyebrows rose a rather large amount.

"I am afraid so."

She lifted her chin in a show of stubborn rebuttal, but said nothing.

"Do you wish to say something in support of Lord Smallwood?" Morley said. "I noticed he captured your exclusive attention the entire time."

"Oh, well, as he should have. He's quite engaging to converse with."

"June, what did he say?" Grace leaned forward in her chair. The others seemed equally eager to hear her report.

"Well, we talked of poetry and literature. Do you know he's read every one of the books we have upstairs?"

"We don't have many." Charity frowned.

"Nevertheless, the ones we do have are my favorites. And he was able to talk of them all, to quote them. We had the most fascinating discussion on the merits of the rhythm of Shakespeare's sonnets."

"Fascinating." Lucy leaned back in her chair in what looked like a frustrated heap.

"What is the matter, Miss Lucy?" Morley was learning more about the female mind the longer he spent with this family.

"Oh, bother. Nothing is the matter. Well, perhaps there is. The whole of it is that I would like to walk with a true gentleman, and though these men were genteel, they certainly talked of themselves an overly large amount."

Morley nodded. "Some men cannot resist the subject."

"Well, I found it tedious after a time. Must they speak only of themselves? I'd like to share some of my thoughts too. But there was never a time, a moment, even when Lord 'I am too big for myself' paused for breath. It seemed as if he spoke on the intake and the out." She fanned herself. "Otherwise the promenade was perfectly lovely. I enjoyed the women we met."

"Oh, yes, I did as well." Charity nodded. "A few said they would come call, and I think perhaps some might share my interests. One certainly wishes to be a writer. The other might just wish to see the cottage. They find us quaint, provincial. Do you know that?"

"Yes, I do." Miss Standish shrugged. "I can't blame them. But perhaps if they stop by, if you call there, they will develop an understanding, a friendship with you which will overshadow our unique circumstance."

"Perhaps. And it might change once we live in the castle, mightn't it?" Charity seemed unusually interested in how they were perceived. He wasn't surprised. She did have a strong desire to converse and defend her opinions.

"It might." June's small smile warmed him and her sisters seemed to rally because of her hope.

Morley turned to Grace. "And how did you find the walk?"

"I think I got a bit too much sun, but otherwise, it was everything I'd hoped. Your tales of the frogs on your land were so diverting my sides hurt from laughing."

Morley grinned. "I am pleased to hear it. Not everyone gets to hear my frog stories, so consider yourself among the few."

Her eyes widened. "Oh, I will, thank you."

"Miss Standish, what more did Lord Smallwood say that leaves such a favorable impression on your mind?"

She looked up, and the small smile on her lips grew which disturbed him further. "I think it was more his manner than anything. He was perfectly attentive, spoke kindly, and praised openly. I found myself refreshed when we were finished." Her eyes stared him down in challenge.

"Pleased I am to hear it is not more than that." Morley straightened his jacket.

"And why should you be pleased about something so completely unrelated to you?" June's eyebrow rose, slowly.

"Because for a moment, I thought he might be among those you hold in greater regard."

"He is." Her words shattered his well being.

"In what way?"

Her eyes flit around them. "I think we should talk about it at a later time."

"But I wish to know." He sounded a bit like a beggar at this point but he didn't care.

The sisters looked back and forth from one to the other until Morley stopped and noted their attention. "Perhaps I might have a word in private?"

"Certainly."

They both stood, and Miss Standish led him outside the front door.

"What is your concern over Lord Smallwood?" She crossed her arms. "You don't like him."

"You are correct."

"And in what manner is this prejudice formed?"

"From my observation of the fellow. Miss Standish, he is the greatest cad I know."

She gasped, and he regretted his brash conversation. But she had to know. At some point he would have had to tell her. It may as well be now.

"He holds little regard for women. He is a rake by reputation, and he says the most inconceivable things when just with the other men. But when he's with the ladies, he finds this inner charm, and that is all that is seen." There, he'd said it.

"Well, I see nothing wrong with that. I appreciate he takes care when he is with the ladies to behave in a manner above his norm. Nothing you have said has yet dimmed my opinion of him."

He was astounded at her words. "And is your opinion so high?"

She looked away. "Well, no."

He breathed out in relief, but she noticed, so she spun back around and stepped closer. "But he is very well growing closer to my estimation of a man I'd like to know."

"I can only hope his true nature will present itself before you are caught in his wiles."

"His wiles?"

"Well, yes."

"And again why should you care? Why have you taken upon yourself this responsibility?"

He opened his mouth and then closed it. "Miss Standish, I just want to see you ladies happy and in good situations. Lord Smallwood hardly fits the recipe."

"And what if we wish to make these sorts of decisions on our own?"

"Do you? I remember clearly you asking for my assistance in this matter. You were certainly willing for assistance in the way of introductions." When she didn't answer, he asked, "Is he coming to call?"

"I imagine he will."

"And you'll receive him?"

"Why wouldn't I?"

"Well, for one, I just told you"—he looked around and lowered his voice—"he's the greatest cad I know."

"And I should base all my opinions of him solely on one individual's assessment?"

"Well, it's a bold accusation, one I do not make lightly." He stepped nearer, suddenly wanting more than anything to impress upon her mind the silliness of such a choice. "You are being incredibly stubborn. Has he...has your heart been captured?"

She rose up on her tiptoes to stand taller next to him. He couldn't help but notice how close her mouth had suddenly come to his own. Her eyes flashed with defiance and he was enticed as much as he was wary. He swayed in place, the very air drawing him closer to her. She opened her mouth to say something. He was entranced, but then she closed it and her shoulders drooped, the very fizzle in the air seemed to fade "My heart is not engaged." She turned away. "Perhaps it is time for you to go?"

He felt too much relief at her statement, and foolishness for pressing her the way he had. He'd never behaved in such an irrational manner. But *Smallwood?* The man's overly satisfied smirk bothered him. "Perhaps it is. I shan't trespass on your kindness any longer today. But I will return to take us all to the assembly?"

"That would be very generous of you. Thank you. And remember we are touring the castle to view the renovations tomorrow. We hope to move in this month." Her voice sounded flat. She didn't look at him when she talked.

"I remember. I shall return for you."

"Or we can meet you there. The walk will do us good."

He dipped his head and bowed. "Until then, Miss Standish." He stepped down their drive, waved to his carriage, and hopped inside before she could do more than simply watch, staring down an empty drive long after he had gone.

Chapter Six

❦

June and her sisters walked into the castle without Lord
Morley. He hadn't shown up this morning by the time they
had scheduled to go, and so they walked without him.

Grace came and stood beside her, close. "I'm sure he
didn't forget us. He'll return."

"Why should I be worried about what Lord Morley does or
doesn't do?"

"He would never forget you, June." Grace squeezed her arm
in such an attempt at comfort, June didn't have the heart to
correct her. Let Grace think what she would. June was not
wasting away in worry that Lord Morley had not shown up. She
wasn't concerned his sudden interest would end, and she most
definitely wasn't feeling the loss of his attention most
keenly. No.

Perhaps her sudden stubborn streak had scared him away.
Why had she been so adamant in favor of Lord Smallwood? He
was handsome. He was a lord. And he was incredibly attentive,
but there had been an air of insincerity which concerned her. It
had been so...pleasant to be doted on. Heady. She would have
walked at his side for many hours more.

They entered through the main front doors of the castle, and the sisters were enchanted. "Ooh, look! They've fixed so many things." Kate pointed to a tapestry hanging on the wall. "Does that look new?"

"It does. I wonder if they've merely washed it."

Charity immediately disappeared down a far hallway. The rest of them made their way into the family living and receiving parts of the castle. Carpets covered the floors. The walls had been cleaned. More candles hung, and the place smelled nice, welcoming.

When they entered their receiving room, June smiled. "Oh, this is lovely." The furniture had been placed in clustered seating arrangements. After the renovations, more light came in through the windows, which were now planed with glass.

"Shall we go and see the bedrooms?" Grace skipped forward.

The sisters climbed a circular, narrow, stone-lined staircase up to the set of family rooms.

Grace ran to her favorite room. Her squeals could be heard down the hallway. June peeked in at her.

"The view is tremendous." Grace stood at the window that overlooked expansive grounds. The women really were gifted a lovely place to live, though unfortunately controlled by careless men who passed the properties around as though they were hotcakes. Hopefully the changing of hands finished with the duke. He seemed determined to care for them, to see them married, and to provide a lovely living situation, if the castle was any indication.

Charity returned. "Everything is much, much better—the kitchens, the stables, even the other rooms--and there's a ball-room." Her eyes were lit with a new happiness, and she seemed suspiciously energetic. June wrapped an arm around her shoulder. "It's going to be a good place for us, then?"

"I believe it will. And there's a lovely music room with a desk. Do you think that could be mine? To write my stories?"

"Absolutely. Is there a schoolroom?"

"Yes, there is, in this wing. But who wants to write their stories in a schoolroom?" Charity made a face.

"Which private quarters is yours?" June walked along the corridor, pleased with their situation—beyond pleased. For the first time in a long time, she had hope things might start to improve.

"I'm down here next to you. I'm assuming you're keeping the master bedrooms to yourself?"

"There has to be some perk to being the oldest spinster sister of the family."

"I don't think spinster status will last long for any of us."

"Don't you?" June searched her face. "I didn't see you and Lord Weatherby making any fast strides in that direction."

"Him? No. He was absolutely pompous and in no way suited for me. But who's to say we have to marry the gentry or even in that class?"

"No one, I suppose, but it is important we always have a place to live, food on the table, and our children provided for." She searched Charity's face. "I believe in love in marriage, but a great deal of unhappiness comes when a family runs out of food."

"Yes, sister. I don't need your lectures. I am merely stating that just because Lord Weatherby and I are not a good match, it doesn't mean there aren't a great deal more people to choose from."

"I have no doubt you shall win over the lot of them." She kissed her sister's face. "Now go see if anything else is needed in your room."

June made her way down to her quarters. She could have put Grace in the room adjoining her own, but instead she might turn it into her own private sitting area. She could put in bookshelves and grow her personal library. If she had a fire going and a comfortable place to sit with a lovely view, she might be happy all her days in this small set of rooms.

She ran her fingers along the tapestries that covered the stone walls. Great attention had been given in all the rooms to make them warmer. Her feet buried in the rugs on the floor. She stepped into the closet that connected the two rooms, and she smiled. Smaller compartments had been added, sections for her clothes, her slippers, and even her jewels, if she had any.

"Gerald and I thought those little extras might be appreciated." Lord Morley's voice startled her so, it initiated a fit of coughing.

"I'm terribly sorry. Here is my handkerchief."

She nodded, took it, and stepped away until her coughing eased. "Oh, my, you startled me. What can you mean, stepping in here without warning?"

"I called to you when I entered your sitting room. You must not have heard."

"No." She dabbed her mouth and then pocketed the handkerchief. "Thank you."

"You are welcome. So, what do you think? I've been anxious to hear if everything is getting completed to your satisfaction."

"Yes, you can tell the duke his work here could not have been gifted to a more grateful family. We are more thankful than he could ever know."

Lord Morley nodded, his expression pleased. "I'm happy to hear it." He led her out of the closet. "Have you searched your rooms? And everything is to your satisfaction?"

"Everything is lovely." They walked out into her room, and she sucked in her breath. "Oh." A large arrangement of flowers had been added to her table, and their lovely mixed-floral scent filled the room. "These are magnificent."

"I thought you'd like them." His voice was quiet.

She turned to him, her eyebrows lifted. "You were right. I am loathe to leave them when no one is staying in this room."

"Well, that's the surprise news. The renovations are complete enough for you to move in. I've arranged for your things to be packed up and moved over today, if you like. You could be sleeping in this room tonight."

"That's wonderful! I—I don't know what to say." Her sudden

desire to throw herself into Lord Morley's arms in a hug of grati-tude warmed her whole room, and she was suddenly acutely aware of their location, alone together.

"Come, we must tell the others." She rushed to the doorway.

"Wait, Miss Standish." His voice, its humility, made her turn.

"Yes?"

"I wanted to—I thought I should—"

She stepped closer.

"I would like to apologize for interfering in your choice of how to spend your time. Even if it would be with someone as loathsome as Lord Smallwood, he would, in fact, be a highly sought after match for most women." His eyes looked away. "I simply seek something infinitely better for you." When his gaze returned, she sucked in her breath at the intensity she saw in his eyes. He stepped closer, capturing her.

Words would not form. Her body hummed in response to his nearness. When he lifted her hand in his own, he brought it to his lips. Her bare skin responded in a cascade of trembles down her arm.

"You are a diamond among women."

His words, his attention, his kindness in helping them move, showered her with a yearning for just such a man in her life, always, and she found herself without words. Nothing would come to mind—nothing except, "You too."

Then she looked away. "I mean, thank you. You're not...a diamond. I mean, you are, but...among men? Is that something men are?" She stepped away and turned her back, wishing to hide at the same time she wished him to stay. "Oh, don't listen to me. I'm just overcome. This is all so wonderful, so good, I don't know what to say." She found his handkerchief and brought it up to her eyes.

The air between them pulled her closer as he stepped up behind. "I'm happy you approve. You and your family deserve to at last be taken care of in the manner you always should have been."

She found the courage to meet his gaze again and was comforted and put at ease. The kindness, the good nature of the man in front of her, made her smile. "I have plans for my sitting room. Books. Music. I shall never have to leave it."

The other sisters came in, and Grace ran to Lord Morley's side. "It's lovely. Is it true? Are we moving in here today?"

"If you like. It's all arranged."

Grace tapped her chin. "Do you think we shall miss that cottage?"

"With its drafts and leaky roof? I think not." Kate shook her head.

"Cook is going to be ecstatic when she sees the kitchen. They've modernized the whole room. It's a cavern now, with every good thing."

"And the ballroom!" Kate held her hands together. "I've heard there's a ballroom."

"Shall we go take a look?" Lucy looked with disapproval from Lord Morley to June and back, which made June smile. "Yes, let's."

The sisters hurried through the hall. Lord Morley offered his arm, which June gratefully took. And soon they were standing in the middle of the ballroom.

"Teach us the waltz." Kate spun. "I shall never know how to place my feet. I shall lose my mind with embarrassment to be held so closely."

"The waltz? Why, it's the easiest of them all. And every man will feel the same when standing so close to you." He bowed to June. "May I?"

She curtsied and tried to pretend she was unaffected. "Of course."

He stepped close, took her hand in his, and placed his other hand on her upper back. "Just so." His face filled with boyish excitement. "And then the music will play in beats of three." He counted. "You move forward or back, to the side and then the opposite, every time. Follow your partner's lead. It's fun, and if you get really good, you hardly notice you're moving. You just sort of...fly."

"Show us!" Grace stepped closer, her eyes intent.

"I can, if you like." He had not released June yet.

June nodded, her heart noticeable in her chest like never before. "I, too, would like to learn."

"So I will count. One, two, three. One, two, three." He stepped forward, and she hurried to follow, stepping back, then to the side, and then together. They repeated the same move again. "And now I shall step back." After practicing a few times, back and then forward, all to the count of three, he started to lead her around the floor.

"What! What are you doing?"

"Don't think. Just move. You've got it."

So she let herself go, following wherever Lord Morley led, spinning and swirling and moving in a glorious count of three she barely noticed. His hand was strong on her back, and the hand that cradled hers was soft, almost an embrace. His eyes were full of signs of caring, interest, happiness.

"Just look at me." He smiled.

Everything in the world seemed to stop, go quiet. She stared up into his eyes, seeing deeper into the man who had done so much for them, seeing beyond his handsome broad jaw and beautiful flecks of green in his eyes, past all of that, to a man whose character made him rise in all estimation. Her breath came faster and she knew she was flushed. But standing so close to such a man...she'd never felt this way before. When at last he paused, she noticed her sisters and the room and how very close she stood to Lord Morley.

Her face heated, and she stepped away. "Thank you. That was...magnificent."

"I wish to have a go." Kate spun. "Teach me."

He bowed to her and took longer on the beginning rudimentary steps. Then he took her in a chaste circle around them.

"Her dance is nothing like yours," Charity whispered in June's ear. "Something tells me you, sister, might be the first to marry."

"What? Hush, now. He's just being kind. He's helping the duke. They're best friends, you know." But she didn't believe the words as they left her lips. Those flowers, his extra attention, their waltz—surely she wasn't the only one feeling something overwhelming between them.

Once they all had a turn practicing the waltz with the patient and willing Lord Morley, he called them to the dining room. "I've asked the kitchen staff if they would prepare a luncheon for us."

"Oh, how lovely. Have we a kitchen staff?" Kate stood closer.

Charity nodded. "We do. Cook is going to love it."

Lord Morley led them to a large room with a grand table in the center.

"What! Where did we get such a lovely table?" Lucy's smile grew the longer they continued.

"We actually discovered it here in the castle." Morley stood taller. "It needed a little care, but I think you will be pleased with the results."

June rushed forward and ran her hand along the soft wood. "It's beautiful. And it will fit us all." She moved to sit.

"No, June. You need to sit at the end."

"What? No, surely." She waved to Lord Morley. "You sit at the end."

"Only if you're at my left."

Her gaze whipped up to his. What did he mean by all this? "Certainly." She dipped her head.

"This is your family, and you are their head. I'm simply here to support you and see you get the care you deserve."

They all took their seats, and a line of servants brought them a delicious simple fare. But they were served, and their cups were filled, and for the first time since her parents died, June felt a measure of ease.

Chapter Seven

Lord Morley eyed his cravat with a far more particular
eye than usual. "Excellent work, Henry."

"Thank you, my lord. Will there be anything else?"

"No. Or perhaps, yes." He stepped back from the mirror and
turned to his valet. "How do I look?"

"Excellent. You never step out of this room less than
excellent."

"I know, and for that, I'm grateful. But what I want to know
now is, how will I look to the ladies?"

Henry lifted his chin and eyed him. "If we are to be about
impressing the ladies, might I suggest the green jacket?"

"Oh, do you think it preferable to the black?"

"I think it better to add color. Green is just a slight deviation
from your usual black and will suit your purposes nicely."

"Good thoughts, Henry. Let's go with the green."

"Very good, my lord." Henry helped him out of the black
jacket and slipped on the green. After brushing it down and
adjusting things only Henry understood, Morley eyed himself
again, pleased.

"Yes, I like this. It does something for my eyes." He turned his head one way, then the other. "Perhaps I should be measured for more jackets of color."

"I quite agree. Shall I schedule an appointment with the tailor here in Brighton?"

"Yes, please do." He dipped his head and then walked out of the room.

He would be attending the assembly with the Standish sisters. Tonight he would inform them of their own visits to the modiste. They must all have new gowns—at least one gown a piece. Gerald had given him the money necessary to take care of all these details. And Lord Morley was left in the awkward position of being their new guardian of sorts, in reality paid for by the duke, and not wanting any of them—particularly June—to feel beholden. At some point, he would need to explain the situation. But there had not yet been a moment where such a conversation would come easily.

Also, he was realizing more and more how much he would welcome a woman to help him pair off the sisters. He needed one of those intrusive mamas of the *ton*, grappling for a lord's attention and keeping the undesirables away. Or even a friend, someone younger. Perhaps Amelia could be persuaded to come, even if Gerald had already declined assistance.

When his carriage pulled in front of the castle, he smiled. How just, how fortunate, the Standish sisters could at last live in their ancestral home, that someone had made right the wrongs of their treatment. He stepped out of the carriage, waiting for the sisters.

Grace hurried out first.

"My dear Miss Grace. Are you to be coming? I thought not..." He frowned. She was far too young to be out in society, and he couldn't be standing at her side the whole night through. Nor could he trust the members of the *ton* to do right by her.

Her pout was obvious as she neared, and her red-rimmed eyes told him what she was about to say. "No, I'm not coming," she said. "Though I think it vastly unfair. I am perfectly happy to sit on the side of the ballroom, to simply watch." She looked up into his face with such sadness he was almost convinced to forgo his night of dancing at the assembly so she could attend with him constantly at her side. But then Miss Standish stepped outside the door, and he forgot all about Grace and her beguiling pout. He stepped closer, his hand outstretched.

Miss Standish's gown shimmered. She wore a lovely green that complimented his own jacket. Although hers was lighter and sparkled somehow, he enjoyed the complimentary hues with his jacket.

"You match." Grace giggled. "You look so well together." Her hands went to her cheeks. "I wish I could remember this vision right here. I wish I could see all the beauty at the assembly." Her pout returned.

"Grace, you shall attend many an assembly when you are old enough."

Morley bowed over Miss Standish's hand. "You look beautiful. Not an eye will be able to look away, including mine." He tried to show his sincerity as he stared into her eyes. Her small smile gave him hope. Perhaps she would see him differently, as someone who wanted to court her. His own thoughts surprised him. The intensity of his feelings seemed to grow with every meeting. Could he convince her of his own worthiness? That was the real question, for he now knew he very much wanted to try.

The other sisters joined them.

He held a hand out, bowing over each. "You all look magnificent. And I heard a rumor we might have some elevated visitors at this smallest of all assemblies."

"Oh?" Lucy's eyes filled with hope. "Who?"

"I have heard the Duchess of York will attend, as well as some very well-connected cousins of hers. They are purported to be handsome." He wiggled his eyebrows.

Charity looked away, apparently not impressed.

But Lucy had stars beaming from her face. "And the duke's son? The Duke of Stratton?"

Every eye turned to her.

"Have you an interest in Lord Felling?" Miss Standish held her hand out to Lucy and guided her and them all toward the carriage.

"I might. I think any son of a duke might be of interest."

"But especially a handsome one?" Kate teased, then adjusted her skirts. "I am most interested in the gowns. I should like to see the fashions we might be gifted next year." Her sigh was almost comical in its dramatic flair.

"That reminds me. The duke has left money aside for a modiste and a new gown for each of you."

Kate clasped her hands together. "I couldn't be happier if someone had gifted me the world." She swayed in her spot.

"Now, don't swoon. Please." Miss Standish and he shared a look. "Let's all get in the carriage," Miss Standish said. "And sit closely, for I don't think Lord Morley should have to ride on top."

"We can all fit, surely. Grace isn't coming."

"Oh, you had to say it." Grace crossed her arms.

"Now, tell the footman to lock the doors. You may entertain yourself in the kitchen or catch up on your reading up in our rooms." Miss Standish smiled and then embraced Grace. "We shall be back, and we will tell you all the lovely sights we see."

"I shall die of boredom with every minute I am left here waiting. Oh, do have fun!"

Lord Morley held Miss Standish's hand as she climbed up into the carriage to join all her other sisters, and then he too alighted. The footman closed their door. He tapped on the roof, and they were off.

He tried not to notice how closely he sat to Miss Standish, but one-half of his body warmed and reminded him with every shift of hers. He cleared his throat. "I should like to dance with each of you. But if a far more handsome man asks you, you may accept his offer. We are, after all, here to introduce you to more of society."

They giggled.

"But I should like to dance first with Miss Standish, if she'll have me."

Her shy dip of her chin charmed him. "Certainly. Thank you for the distinction."

The carriage ride was all too short for Morley, but each sister seemed more than anxious to exit and attend.

"Have you been to an assembly here before?"

"We have, but never in so much splendor. Thank you." Miss Standish placed her hand on his arm.

When the footman opened their carriage door, Morley hopped out and helped each of the girls down. "And now we shall be about the introductions." He grinned, and they all entered the assembly hall together.

As soon as they walked in the door, two girls ran forward and clasped the hands of Lucy and Kate. Pleased, Morley smiled down at Miss Standish. "I'm happy to see they will have friends here."

"You have undertaken quite a harrowing job, escorting a family of four sisters to an assembly."

"At least you are all sensible and can be trusted to make good choices."

Her eyebrow lifted.

He hurried to add, "And can well make decisions for your own welfare."

She laughed. "I wanted to apologize. I do thank you for your concern and for your insight."

"Pleased I am to hear it. But I have learned my lesson. I will not interfere on your behalf unless the situation turns dire."

"And what would constitute dire? I'm all ears." Her face said she was teasing, the rise of one corner of her mouth, her brilliant eyes dazzling sparkles of light at him. But he could only think of about one hundred scenarios that would be considered dire in his book.

Lord Smallwood approached and bowed. "I am so pleased you have come. Might I have our dance?"

The music began, and Miss Standish started. "Oh! Lord Smallwood. I have promised the first to Lord Morley, but I can save you the second?"

Morley's triumph beamed out his eyes as he noted the narrowed expression on Lord Smallwood's face.

But Smallwood just bowed. "Certainly. I will be counting the beats until it is our turn." He turned from them without another look at Morley, who couldn't help but chuckle.

"My, we've upset his sensibilities."

"You don't look at all unhappy to have done so."

"Of course I'm not." He paused. "But are you? Would you rather dance the first with him?" His heart shuddered at the thought.

But Miss Standish shook her head. "No, of course not. I have agreed to this set with you. And you've done so much to help us. I'm pleased to take the first." But her expression clouded, and he wished to wash the line of concern from her brow. "Do you think he is very much disappointed?"

"Lord Smallwood?" Morley glanced over at him. His sullen expression and crossed arms did give rise to some evidence he was displeased. "He does look a bit unraveled, but never fear. You shall dance away his worries in the second set. This, Miss Standish, is what happens to all lords during a dance. They can't have every woman they desire at the exact moment they wish to dance with her, and it unsettles the more competitive among us."

She seemed a bit mollified. "And they don't give up? They still return their attentions?"

Her great concern about Smallwood's attentions was in no small way disturbing to Morley, but he merely nodded. "You will be so surprised to note when a lord cannot have the attention he seeks, he will only up his efforts to win her favor. The more difficult a woman is to woo, the harder a man will work."

She considered him and then nodded. "I find some of this very tedious."

His laugh carried to those around them. "So soon?"

But when he saw she was the utmost serious, he amended his expression. "I, too, find it tedious. I much prefer the honest and open declarations between two people."

They joined a line of guests, and he startled. "I have not been paying attention. Are your sisters dancing?"

"Oh, Lord Morley. You have taken on a large task indeed. They are dancing—all but Charity, who is in the corner in a heated discussion, no doubt about the merits of the war against Napoleon."

Morley followed her gaze, and sure enough, Miss Charity had collected quite a circle of men, all intent on her words.

"I've never seen the like."

"I'm not surprised, for you've never seen Charity. The man she marries will be of a different sort, I'm certain."

"Or the very powerful sort. Only someone of great stature or confidence could rise to be her equal."

Miss Standish grew quiet, so he returned his gaze to find her openly appreciative. "You are everything this family needs. Thank you again for your great kindness."

"I do not do all these things simply for kindness's sake."

"You don't?" Her eyes smiled at him.

The music started, and they were presenting to each other and to their opposites. He cursed the dance he had at first so strongly desired. For he wished to tell Miss Standish exactly why he was assisting her and her sisters, and his reasons had very little to do with the winning of his game of cards.

But he smiled and went through the motions, not holding Miss Standish's hands nearly long enough as they passed each other in the set.

When it was over, he almost offered to go for a walk, but Lord Smallwood arrived and took her from him to the maddening sounds of the waltz.

Lucy stood at his side.

He reached out a hand. "Would you care to dance?"

"Yes, I could only dance the waltz with you at this point."

"Very good. I shall keep it simple and easy."

"And as you are most interested in my sister, I won't have to worry you might attempt something improper."

He coughed. "Certainly not. And how do you know anything about me being most interested in the lovely Miss Standish?"

"We all know it. For why else would you show such interest? Why would you help with the castle, pay for so many things, offer your carriage?" She placed her hand on his shoulder. "You are planning to court her, are you not?"

He was completely unsettled for many reasons, the first of which being he began to understand the consequences of not explaining to the sisters he was, in fact, their benefactor. It gave rise to some sudden misunderstandings between them.

The second thing he wished to do was to affirm her assumption his interests in Miss Standish were very much of the romantic sort. But the other thing which must be known was she clearly was not as interested in him. And so the topic should not be broached in so open a manner.

But as they concentrated on dancing the waltz, he couldn't say any of the things required to be said. He didn't know how to begin.

"I shall have a conversation with all of you sisters tomorrow when I come to call, how does that sound?"

Her small smile looked a little too victorious, but she nodded and said, "I shall be anxious to receive your call."

When their dance completed, he asked Miss Kate, and then Miss Charity, who was loathe to leave her conversation—and the men were loathe to lose her.

"Come now, you must dance."

"Why must I dance?" She curtsied in front of him, and he bowed.

"Because we are not simply here for you to have enlivening

conversation." He narrowed his eyes. "What were you discussing?"

"All manner of things. Most of them are Tories and therefore daft."

"Miss Charity, you cannot speak so."

"Are you a Torie, then, as well?"

"I am not."

Her face lit. "I'm so happy to hear it. Then you will appreciate we cannot possibly be taxing the poor in increasing amounts and expect them not to starve."

"Miss Charity, have you read any good poetry lately?"

"Poetry?" She frowned. "Oh, as in my lessons with June?" She sighed. "Yes, I've been reading sonnets."

Relieved to have found a safer subject, he nodded with encouragement. "And do you have a favorite?"

She humored him and talked of niceties for the remainder of the dance. But after she curtsied to him, she hurried back to her corner of the room.

Morley was in desperate need of some feminine help for these ladies.

"You have your hands full, Morley." Her velvet voice itched on his skin, but he was relieved to hear it nonetheless.

"Annabelle. Lady Annabelle." He bowed over the hand of an old childhood friend.

"Oh, we needn't be so formal." Her blonde hair was piled high on her head, her dress fit snugly about her waist, and her smile was as lovely and as broad as ever.

"It's good to see you. I didn't know you were here in Brighton." He hadn't seen her in months, when he'd stepped away from her due to her misunderstanding of possible romantic inclinations on his part. He had hoped to sever ties completely and stem off any gossip that might start or speculation that might arise.

"I had to come. It's all over the *ton* what you are doing for the

Sisters of Sussex. Tell me, Morley, did you really win them in a game of cards?"

Music for another waltz began, so he bowed. "Dance with me?"

Her eyes widened, but then she smiled. "Of course."

He led her out to the floor. "How much is the news being tossed around—that I won them in a game of cards?"

She studied him. "I heard it from Lord Smallwood, but he seems totally enamored with the eldest."

"It's not something I'd like repeated, for their sake."

She tipped her head. "Do you feel some sort of protective care over them? As if they are wards or something?"

"I believe I do. I inherited their property. You can't just kick out a family of women. And the duke provided plenty of money to get them started. I'd like to do well by them."

"Most people would keep them in their cottage, send them an allowance, and be done with them. Do you really think the *ton* will accept them back as equals after they've been nearly destitute for so long?"

The music paused, and the Master of Ceremonies announced, "Her Grace, the Duchess of York."

Then the music started back up, but the duchess went straight to Miss Standish and kissed her cheeks.

"I think they have connections enough. You know they are distant relatives of the royal household?"

She sighed. "You have a personal interest in this situation."

"I—" He looked away, regretting ever asking her to dance. "I don't know what I have, except mostly a sense of responsibility to see them in good situations. Whatever you can do to help by limiting gossip would be most appreciated."

She studied him. "Word has spread already. If others talk, it won't be my doing."

His heart sank. If people were talking, word would get back to the sisters. The Standishes were all engaged in pleasant diversions, as far as he could tell. Lord Smallwood was waiting off the ballroom floor while Miss Standish danced with another—an older, widowed gentlemen with three children. Charity was dancing. He was pleased to see it, and by the slight blush to her face, she might be as well. He chuckled. Lucy was dancing with the son of a Marquess. Yes, her sights were high. And he was a decent enough chap, if not a bit boring. And Kate...his gaze flitted about the room, looking for Kate. She was dancing as well, but with Weatherby.

"Have you accounted for all your chicks?" Lady Annabelle's eyebrow rose. "Really, Morley, I never took you for the mother hen type."

"I need your assistance."

"And why would I give it?" Her lips pressed together in a thin line.

"I know things didn't progress between us, but have compassion. A man cannot do this all by himself."

"I think they are very much in hand with Miss Standish at the helm, are they not? With elevated friendship from more than one duchess? Where is the Duke of Granbury? He and his wife will come assist, will they not?"

"I don't know. I shall write directly." If Lady Annabelle couldn't be persuaded to assist, he would find another. His first plan would be to tell the sisters exactly what his role was in their lives.

The set came to a close, and he led Lady Annabelle off the floor.

Before he could turn to find the sisters, Miss Standish approached with fire in her face. "How could you?" Tears welled in her eyes before she turned away. "We're going home with Lord Smallwood."

Morley held the side of his cheek with one hand, while Smallwood's smirk ignited his irritation.

"Wait."

She stopped.

"Just like that?" They were attracting all kinds of unwanted attention. He considered their reputation and said, "Could we converse, please? With your sisters?"

She shook her head. "Come calling at the cottage. That is where you will find us."

"What? That's just asking to be uncomfortable."

"I have nothing more to say to you." She lifted her chin. "Goodbye." Then she turned from him.

Lady Annabelle's face filled with amusement. Most everyone else refused to meet his gaze. He went to glower in the corner.

He couldn't leave—not until he knew the women were home safely. Would Smallwood get them home? Yes. But he still couldn't just leave them without his added eye at the assembly.

He leaned back against the wall and considered his mess of a life more trying than any of his acquaintance. And he had only Gerald to blame for it—and himself. He could have simply told the women upon their first acquaintance. He hadn't kept the knowledge from them, precisely, but he'd enjoyed their pleased surprise when they thought he was paying a social call. He'd been astonished at how much he'd enjoyed the idea of simply expressing an interest in a woman. But in truth, he wouldn't have done so had he not felt a responsibility toward them.

And the truth had now come to haunt him.

Chapter Eight

A s Lord Smallwood handed her down, he murmured, "I've heard tell he won monies from the duke with which to provide for your family. Why not enjoy better circumstances? I would live here at the castle and be happy." He placed his lips on the back of her hand. "If I might, I'd like to come call on you?"

She dipped in a curtsy. "I'd like that, thank you."

Lord Smallwood left in his carriage. They entered the castle to the sounds of loud laughing and uproarious playing of the piano.

They moved quickly to the music room to find Lord Morley dancing as if with a partner and Grace at the piano playing faster and faster, watching Lord Morley try and keep up.

June winced. "What are you doing here?" When they didn't hear, she walked to the piano. "What are you doing here?" With hands on hips, she frowned in his direction.

Grace's mouth dropped, and she stopped playing. "What are you doing, June? This is Lord Morley."

"Yes, I'm painfully aware of who is in my home uninvited. I wish he would take his deception elsewhere."

Grace's face clouded in confusion.

"I have not deceived anyone."

"On, no? Then why do I have to learn at the assembly you won guardianship of our family at a card table? Not just once, but many times over I was favored with the story. 'Strapped him with five destitute sisters. Thought he was winning big when he really inherited a nightmare.'" She crossed her arms. "I think we've had enough of your pretend offers of friendship. I'm sorry you are strapped with us, but we shall try to eat as little as possible." She moved to the door, gesturing for him to leave. "Now, if you'll excuse us?"

Lord Morley moved slowly toward the door. "You are repeating back what the vicious mouths of the *ton* will repeat, but it is not the truth, nor is it what happened. Might I please explain?"

"Yes, June, let him explain." Charity moved to stand beside June.

"I should like to hear all sides of the story." Lucy nodded.

More out of pure exhaustion than anything, June waved him toward the sofa. "Please hurry. We are all anxious for our beds."

"I will not detain you for more than a brief moment." He cleared his throat.

The sisters all took seats. Each one looked concerned. Grace seemed hurt. June supposed everyone was, but Grace knew how to hide it least.

"I did indeed win this castle, the surrounding land, and the cottage in a game of cards, as well as a significant amount of money."

"But why was our castle part of a card game?" Kate's eyebrows furrowed together.

"Why would the duke try to be rid of us?" Grace held her hands clasped tightly together in her lap, and June wished to spare her sisters some of the reality of their situation, but she supposed it must all be spoken.

"The Duke of Granbury's actions make him sound uncaring or negligent, but I think on the contrary—he has some plan to bring us all together, and he purposely lost to me."

"So he wanted to foist us off on you?" June looked away. "You particularly."

"I thought the duke liked us, trusted us." Grace looked like she might start crying.

Lord Morley leaned forward. "He most absolutely does. He doesn't think things through at times, and this is one of those times when I wish he'd done more than simply lose the properties. But to his credit, he wrote me a letter with strict instructions as to your welfare, down to the specific renovations necessary for the castle, the modiste visits for you ladies, how soon he would like you to move in...all of it. In all of my actions I have been honest, as I never corrected you in assuming the duke was doing all of this for you. It was he. It *is* he. I am here as the owner. You are my tenants. And I and he believe in caring for our tenants. I am not of the mind your illustrious family should be left destitute on the very property which should be yours by right, simply because you are women and have lost your father—forgive my bluntness. Nor do I think you should be without protection. The *ton* would agree with me. They've shown their care for you in the many visits and the great distinction they've consistently shown you."

"But it puts us in a lower standing—subjects us to ridicule." June frowned deeper.

"It might from those of lesser stature, but any of your truly equal birth and pedigree will think only of your unfortunate hard times and consider you as peers. Think of the Duchess of York, for example."

"She is a dear," Kate sighed.

Lord Morley looked at each of the sisters in turn and kept his last lingering gaze on June. "Please do not let this deter our friendships, the close manner in which we have been able to associate. I've not had this much enjoyment in years. And I've come to care for you all and to want to be near you." He moved closer to June. "I had hoped you and I—"

"And that is where this conversation must stop. You cannot think we can continue on the same vein. Before we thought you a generous friend who might have an interest in knowing us better, but now we know the truth. You have behaved as such only out of duty and obligation." She felt the corners of her mouth drop and shake. No, she must not cry in front of this man. "And that is the worst of it all. No one likes to feel beholden, and Lord Morley, that is how we feel every day of our lives. We continue on, because we have no other choice, but our dearest friends will be those to whom we owe nothing. I'm sure you understand." She stood.

"And this is how it is to be?"

"I believe it must."

"Might I still come to call?"

"Certainly. Come to see the progress of your investments. Come to step in on your tenants, but it is with the accurate understanding we now all share that we will move forward in our relationship with you."

"Can we not return?"

June shook her head.

Lord Morley stood, the very energy which typically held him tall and vibrant in any room seemed to have drained from his person. "I am deeply saddened to hear this."

"I regret it must be so." June lifted her chin, refusing to be influenced, though a part of her rebellious heart wanted to break. Her sisters stood as he trudged slowly out of the room.

Once he was well and truly gone, Lucy clucked. "You needn't have been so harsh."

Charity shook her head. "She must. No one can fall in love with someone who controls everything in their life."

June was struck by her sister's words—fall in love. "I wasn't falling in love."

"Of course not. Not when he owns everything around us." Charity moved toward the family rooms. "I do like living here. I'm happy we aren't moving back to the cottage."

"Would that we could. Would that we could move far away where we know no one, where we earn our stay, and pay for our own rent."

"And how would we ever manage such a thing?" Lucy shook her head. "We cannot earn money. This is precisely what our great uncle would have wished. We honor him by accepting gratefully all of the aid we do from those around us. It is because of him and his ancestry we are thus honored."

"You are wise, Lucy. Too wise. For some of them do nothing but mock us. Honor has nothing to do with it."

"But those people don't have to be our friends, now, do they?" Charity brushed them away, running her hand through the air.

"I don't suppose they do, no."

"We shall return to the local society. We shall stand proudly in our heritage." Lucy smiled.

"Shall we still have a visit from the modiste?" Kate's eyes, full of hope, melted a bit of June's stubbornness.

"Of course we shall."

"Then I am as pleased as anyone." Kate turned to June. "Though I had hoped you and Lord Morley would make something of this together. He is the dearest man."

"Yes, he is." Grace's lip extended. "And you interrupted the most jovial game. He was pretending—"

"Yes, we saw what he was doing." Charity stood. "I believe I shall find my bed."

The others joined her, all but June. "Good night, dear sisters. Good will come of this somehow. We shall see evidence of it. Perhaps near the end of our days, but it shall be there."

"Perhaps sooner than you think." Kate kissed the top of her head, and the others made their way upstairs.

June sat staring into the flames at the fireplace until they turned to embers. She *had* hoped for something more with Lord Morley. For the first time, she'd seen the potential for real happiness there. Was she now left at the mercy of men like Lord Smallwood? Gentlemen in name only, pretty with their words, but none of it meaning anything? She supposed she was.

Chapter Nine

Morley penned a rather vicious letter to Gerald: "As your ill-used friend, I request your and the duchess's immediate assistance in this matter. Yours, etc."

But he supposed his old friend deserved a talking down. He'd meddled too close to the mark, strapped Morley with a huge responsibility, and then the very meddling meant to draw him closer to June had been the force to drive her away.

Once they arrived, Morley could return to London.

The real problem with all of it was Morley's loss of his much-cherished peace of mind. Before these last few weeks in Brighton, he'd been perfectly content with his life, perfectly pleased to spend his days how he wished. If he had a moment of quiet, his mind wandered to poetry or literature or considerations on which horse to buy. He would drop in to see his mother. He aided his friends—mostly Gerald, if he was being honest—and had a supreme existence.

But now? He ran an agitated hand through his hair. Now he was doomed to this consistent unease, this pinch in his core, that refused a moment's rest, that fixated wholeheartedly with a grip of steel on thoughts of June. Since she had most decidedly shut him out of her life, every waking minute of the day was now plagued with loss, sorrow, and desperation. Two times he'd stopped himself from riding back over to the castle in the middle of the night. Two times he'd paced the floor, seeking a solution to his new mess of an existence. And he'd found no solution.

Escape. He must leave. And Gerald must come. With those thoughts, he'd found a sad sort of melancholy to allow sleep, and had dozed off in the night.

And now, with the letter in the hands of an express rider, he drank himself some fortitude as he prepared to deliver a modiste to the castle. He needn't accompany. Or perhaps he would busy himself on the unfinished parts of the castle, talking with the workmen and getting a better idea of when the work would finish.

What was he to do with a fixed and furnished castle? That was a problem for another day. For now, he was off to pick up Marguerite, the best modiste in Brighton, or so he'd heard.

He stepped back from the door, surprised, as a woman bustled toward him with a shopkeeper behind. Books of fabric, rolls of the stuff, a box of who knew what, and a robust, energetic woman all climbed into his carriage.

After he'd joined her, he smiled at a young man and woman. "I am Lord Morley. You must be..."

"Miss Marguerite, and this is Thomas. Five sisters, you say?" She fanned herself. "Pleased I am to help with the Standish sisters. I've heard tell of them these years past. Such a sad tale, to be left as they were, when their uncle was so fond, when the old duke himself would have rolled in his grave to know his line had diminished thus." She dabbed her eyes. "It is an honor to be dressing them."

Lord Morley nodded. "They are most grateful."

"And if they spread it far and wide who it was they chose, I'll add in some extras—a morning dress and another ball gown, perhaps. I'd like to be known as the modiste for their family."

She eyed him and then looked away. "Are you the one who will be paying for their purchases?"

"I am."

"Do you have a particular interest in these women?" Her eyebrows lifted, and Lord Morley was astounded at the brash question.

"They are my tenants. And while they weren't heir to a great deal of pin money, I and the Duke of Granbury wish to remedy the situation. In a sense, I view them as in my care, but not in any other manner to which you might be referring."

She sniffed. "It's an important question to ask, as unpleasant as it might be. I shall be making up dresses for young debutantes, then, if I am to understand?"

"Yes, certainly. We are seeking matches for them all."

She nodded.

Rattled by the woman's wholly brash line of questions, Lord Morley tried to talk of trivial matters until they pulled up in front of the castle. "And here we are. One more thing I'd like to address. The eldest, Miss Standish—she will see to it her sisters are to be the most carefully and beautifully cared for, but I would like you to order an extra gown for her, spend the most on her necessities, and in all ways ensure she is treated as well as or greater than the others."

Her eyebrows rose, but she wisely said nothing.

To stem gossip, he added, "Remember, she is the eldest."

"Ah, understood. I shall do my best. These women will be the most finely appointed, mark my words."

"Thank you. Your reputation precedes you. I would expect nothing less."

Kate met them at the door, and Lord Morley had to smile. The woman cared more for fashion than for the men at the balls. Perhaps she would enjoy learning to be a seamstress. He would look into it for her.

He stood next to his carriage, watching the busy front door of the home, the entrance of the modiste, and listening to the excited chatter just inside the door. June stepped into his line of sight, noticed him, and then backed away. His hands flexed opened and closed three times, and then he entered the castle. He could do this. They'd hardly spent enough time together for him to be so fascinated with the woman. His interest would ebb, and he would be able to continue on in a normal fashion.

Once he was certain she had moved on to another room in the house, he made his way to the opposite side of the immense castle. The building was an architectural wonder. Large turrets, thick walls, and rooms all around enclosed a center courtyard. And it was in this courtyard he would like to employ gardeners to make the place beautiful again. There was soil—a tree or two, even. But Morley would like to see benches, a fountain, hedges, roses, arbors—the place could be an oasis. And it would not draw the heat on summer days if it had more greenery and some shade. Perhaps when the sisters were all gone and married, he could come stay here for half of the year. It was becoming an impressive structure once again.

As he walked to the furthest end, he inspected some of the stonework. The bricklayers and stonemasons Gerald employed worked night and day to make the place fully secure and only accessible through the front door. The sisters were likely unaware, but Morley had also employed extra footmen as security at all hours, the men specifically placed so the sisters would be protected.

As he made his way back to the lived-in part of the house, he couldn't help but feel pleased. At least the structural parts of his obligations were going well and on schedule. And the personal aspect—the sisters—they were doing well also. The brief conversation that they had been acquired by a bet would not affect them long, not when so many others were in support. They were lovely, each one of them beautiful, and he knew they could overcome such a thing. Or he hoped. He awaited further insight from the duke, should Gerald care to give it.

A rider came running into the courtyard. "I'm looking for the Earl of Morley."

"I am he."

He leapt off his horse. "I await a reply."

"Very good."

Morley opened the seal. It was from Gerald.

We shall come. Announce the girls' dowries. Five thousand a piece."

Five thousand a piece. Morley pressed his mouth together. That was astounding. Gerald was a good man. Despite his eccentricities, he'd been through great sorrow. He deserved his newfound happiness and had learned to show great compassion to others.

He handed payment to the rider. "Please tell the duke I look forward to his arrival. There is room at the castle, if he so desires."

The rider nodded and took off running.

And Morley was almost free of them. His breath left slowly as he sought the great relief and peace that must come from such an acknowledgment. But his heart stayed tight, his lungs constricted. At least the girls would now be able to easily overcome whatever stigma came from being won by a bet, from being of good name and penniless. He could wash his hands of the whole situation, if he wished it.

Memories of Grace, urging him on to silliness, thoughts of Lucy and her overly conscientious adherence to propriety, Kate's love for fashion, and Charity... he hadn't totally figured out the reasons for Charity's eccentricity, but he was intrigued. Thoughts of them all filled his mind with a poignant sadness at his loss. His mind fought against thoughts of June, but they came anyway. June, the woman who had maintained such a lovely family while neglected and quite possibly hungry. His lips tugged in a small smile. She was remarkable.

And very much disgusted with him.

He brushed his hands as if to shake thoughts of them away. If only such an action would, in fact, succeed. Then he headed in the direction of their front room. He remembered a book or two on the tables.

Well into a new novel, *Sense and Sensibility*, he counted himself lucky to at least not be as daft as this man, Edward. "Get some sense, man."

"I must admit I'm surprised to see you here." Lord Smallwood sauntered into the room, and Morley wanted to push him right back out the door.

"I could say the same of you, even more particularly, since I own the place."

"Ah, so now you admit it."

"I never denied it."

He sat across from Morley and crossed one leg. "I enjoy her, Morley. I wonder if I might find something, some kind of happiness with her I've never found anywhere else."

Morley refused to answer.

"You don't believe me."

"I know how disdainful you can be. I've yet to see this be any different from any other of your conquests. Know this: broken hearts in this family will be answered. These sisters are not without friends."

"You've made that clear. Though I'm not certain of your emotional engagement here. Are you tied to these women? Just why are you so intent on aiding the family?"

"Lord Smallwood?" June hurried into the room. "I just heard you were here." She approached and reached out with both hands to Smallwood. She glanced at Morley out of the corner of her eye as she passed. "Morley."

She'd called him "Morley." That, at least, was something. Morley, the name his dearest friends called him. The name he'd used before the title was even his, as a promise with his best friend, who, ironically, he'd called Granbury before the Gerald became the duke and only Gerald now that he was the duke. Even though she probably did it without thinking, it made him feel closer to her.

"Hello, Miss Standish. I trust your visit with the modiste is going well?"

She turned briefly to him. "Yes, it is. We will have to thank His Grace when he arrives."

"Is the Duke of Granbury coming, then?" Smallwood smiled in her direction, and Morley wanted to wipe the expression from his face.

"Yes, he and his wife." She slipped a hand on Smallwood's arm. "Now, did you want to take the tour?"

"I would be most intrigued to see this most mysterious of all castles. It has been closed for years."

"It's lovely now. We will be very happy here." They walked out of the room without another look in his direction.

And Morley supposed this was the way of things between him and Miss Standish now.

The modiste bustled her way back out to the main receiving area of the home, and the servants assisted her into his carriage. Before he himself climbed up, Miss Charity ran out to greet him.

"Lord Morley."

Relieved at the cheerful greeting, he said, "Yes? How was your visit?"

"Oh, I'll look stunning, as expected." Miss Charity waved her hand as though such a thing mattered little.

Morley could only smile, because as beautiful as she was, the gowns would only draw further attention.

"Thank you. I wanted to thank you. June is...well, she's stubborn and prideful. So I don't know if you'll ever get another kind word from her, but the rest of us think you're smashing."

He raised an eyebrow.

"'Smashing' isn't at all the word, is it?" Charity shrugged. "It sounds right in my head, but off my lips...perhaps too much?"

"I hear it most often at Jackson's or with the gentlemen on a hunt."

"Hmm. Are there any good words for a lady?" Charity tapped her chin.

"Good words?"

"Yes, truly exclamatory or descriptive. I feel men have taken all the good ones."

He tipped back his head, a laugh rumbling up inside him. Then he shook his head. "I'm afraid we have stolen all the good ones, yes. So around me, you may use the word 'smashing.'"

"Just right. So, anyway, the sisters and I—not June—have been talking, and we would like you to come to dinner."

"Oh? When?"

"Tonight. Every night. We want you around. And even if June doesn't allow it, we don't care what she thinks. In this instance, she's wrong. You've become family. So please come tonight. And we will keep inviting you. Come as often as you like or you can." She rocked back on her heels. Morley could see it took something for her to extend the invitation, as if she were afraid he would turn her down.

"Absolutely. There is no family I would wish to dine with more. Expect me this evening. And for as many evenings in which we are not engaged."

"Thank you. We shall all be glad to have you. Even June, though I doubt she'll let you know."

"Either way, perhaps I can somehow show her my sincerity. I'd like us to be on good terms, at least."

"And so would we." She whipped around. "See you tonight." Her hurrying feet back into the castle made him smile. Then she paused. "I know you are escorting Miss Marguerite home, but Lord Smallwood is hereabouts. I'm not certain they should be without escort." She winked and entered the castle.

Chapter Ten

Not without escort.

He moaned. Could the sisters not follow Miss Standish and Smallwood around and act as an escort of sorts? Did he really wish to insert himself, to be seen even more as a bother in her life?

He considered Smallwood in there working his charms, his open smiles that hid his real intentions, and the thought settled things. He called up to his coachman, "Please take Miss Marguerite back to her establishment, and then return for me here."

"Very good, my lord." The coachman nodded, and the carriage was sent on its way.

He turned back to the house. Even if June never again saw him as someone she would want to spend her time with as an equal, he certainly could insert himself between her and Smallwood. No matter what the man said, Morley couldn't help but doubt his sincerity.

He picked up his pace, pushed through the front door, and marched through the entry.

Charity was already upstairs, looking out over a balcony that surrounded the front entry. She pointed toward the back end of the courtyard and then waved.

He nodded and moved in the identified direction. And in good time. Smallwood had stepped closer to Miss Standish and was involved in what looked like a serious discussion. Alone. Where were her sisters? A footman? A maid? Did no one care for propriety in this home?

"Ah, there you are." He lifted a hand to them.

Miss Standish jerked up her head and took a step back.

Excellent.

Smallwood frowned at him.

When he was close enough to converse, Miss Standish spoke. "Was there something we needed to address?"

"As a matter of fact, yes."

She waited. "We are all ears. What was it that needed to be addressed right in this moment?"

"I felt this moment an excellent one to address any manner of things, as I happened upon a situation which merited a chaperone."

Miss Standish sucked in her breath. "Surely you can see we are in the center of the house, visible to all."

"Hmm." He dipped his head. "Nevertheless, there is some stonework I wish for you to inspect so we might have your final approval on coloring and placement."

"Coloring and placement? Of the stone?"

"Yes, the masons don't want to continue until they know you are in agreement with the slightly different shades, the natural variances which occur with...rocks." He cleared his throat.

Smallwood adjusted his coat. "Shall I attend as well?"

"If you would like, though I hardly think this activity sounds riveting."

"True, but one could not leave you unchaperoned at any rate, either." Smallwood raised his eyebrows in challenge.

Miss Standish's tired sigh would have made Morley laugh at

any other time, but today he felt only sadness he would vex her so. But what more was he to do? There were plenty of men she could accept attention from who would be far superior to Small-wood. If Morley was to aid her in finding a match, it would not be to this cad.

They moved in the direction from which he had come, though he knew the effort to be pointless. But he grinned anyway. "The stone was taken from the same quarry, therefore, the same rock as the original. I find that interesting. If you think about it, quite romantic as well. For the same ocean crashed on these rocks, the same time period of people stepped upon them. Hundreds of years in these walls and in the earth, separated for a time, and now they are combined anew."

Smallwood snorted.

They moved along the wall. Morley reached out to trail his fingers on the stone. "So this stone right here is easily two hundred years old, which, by the way, is as long as a member of your family has owned or been associated with this castle."

June said nothing, but his heart warmed when her fingers reached out to touch the stone. "Just think who else has touched this very wall."

He led her further along. "If you remember, this part of the castle was in shambles. A large portion of the wall up here had even crumbled. And that was the part we wanted to complete with some urgency. You will see it is now secure, but a few remaining touches are left." They approached the far wall. "And though it is very important you are secured in your home, the difference in coloring on the stone gave us pause. What say you?"

He stepped back and held out a wall sconce, the light helping them see shades of rock and patterns.

Smallwood could not look more irritated, but Miss Standish approached, studying the stone. "So, this is the same age as the other stone in the castle."

"Yes, that is correct. If you see this line, this is where the masons collected stone from the nearby areas, the same general location of the other stone, but it has since been subject to wind and rain and sun."

She ran her hands along the rock in such a reverent manner, Morley was pleased he had suggested such a task.

"I can see the different colors and the discontinuity, but perhaps unlike some others, I love the story it tells and find it charming." She turned to him, her eyes bright, interested. "You may tell the head mason I am happy with his efforts and he may continue the same in other areas which require repair."

"I will indeed." He considered her. "I would think you'd like to be more involved in these sorts of decisions."

"Yes, I would."

"Then it shall be done."

The happiness that lit her face taught him a plethora of new things about this fascinating woman. Her desire to be independent was not merely an expression or a matter of pride. She'd been solely in charge of her family, in caring for them, despite the interference of many men like himself. And she felt more comfortable in that position. To her credit, he'd never met a woman so wholly focused on anyone besides herself.

Then Smallwood stepped up beside her. "I do think, perhaps, it is disconcerting to see the break in the wall, to see the line of rebuild."

She shook her head. "No, that is the part I find most fascinating."

"Hmm. Perhaps if a true masonry expert were to be assisting here instead of the amateurs doing this work, it would have been completed differently."

"My lord?" Mr. Smithson approached from behind.

"Ah, perfect timing," Morley said. "Miss Standish, I would like you to meet the leading mason in London, who the Duke of Granbury cajoled into helping us."

She turned and reached out her hands.

Smallwood scowled.

"Your work is fantastic. I most appreciate the delicate respect and balance you have shown in the history of our home and in the surrounding nature."

"Ah, a woman who appreciates our efforts."

"This is Miss Standish. She and her sisters are the tenants here. The castle has been in her family since it was built."

"We discovered something you might find interesting." He rounded the corner and came back with his rucksack. "The boys picked this up while we were cleaning out the rubble. It looks to be something the family might have hidden in the rocks."

Miss Standish gasped beside him and stepped closer.

Mr. Smithson pulled out a small chest. "It has a lock. But it seems to be very old." He gently handed it to her.

"Thank you." The reverence with which she took the chest into her arms pulled at Morley's heart, and he suddenly wanted to know her whole story—the history of her family and why she and the sisters were in their situation.

They made their way further along the hall. "Tell me, Mr. Smithson, what else are your men working on?"

They talked together, which left Smallwood and Morley standing side by side.

"I know what you're doing," Smallwood mumbled.

"Pardon?"

He looked away. "What if I'm sincere? What if you're intruding on a great opportunity for her?"

Morley considered his words. "Then she will know, won't she? I'll not stand in the way of her choices."

"Just in my ability to convince her."

"Just in your complete disregard for propriety." He tried to relax but everything about Smallwood set his teeth to grinding.

"Hmm. And your own?"

What an absurd assessment. "We always have the sisters with us, the servants, the workers."

He nodded. "Regardless. Do you not think it quite outside your role to be so attentive? I'll tell you, I care little about your sensibilities. I don't see you as a guardian. She certainly doesn't. And I have little regard for your mother hen picking stipulations about time spent with Miss Standish."

Morley stopped him and let the other two go further ahead. "You need to care about my sensibilities. For each of these sisters is in my safekeeping, and they will be treated with respect by true gentlemen." He stood taller. "They are not without friends."

Morley held Smallwood's gaze until he nodded. Then they continued walking.

After much longer than Morley anticipated, Miss Standish finished talking with Mr. Smithson. They planned for some extra work to be done up in one of the towers and for a fountain to be added to the courtyard, among other things.

When at last she turned to him and was ready to make her way back to the living areas of the castle, Lord Smallwood had checked his timepiece three times.

"I shall be off. But will I be seeing you at the ball in the pavilion?"

"The ball?" She looked at Morley and back. "I—believe so?"

"Excellent. Might I secure a set with you there?"

"Certainly. Allow me to walk you out." She lifted her chin. "If our chaperone would allow a moment?"

"Oh, of course. I'll be watching from here." He pointed to the front entry and the clear view he had from where he stood to the door.

"Thank you." She paused, then handed him the chest. "Would you hold this?"

He cradled it. "Yes."

Could they manage to be friends, on good terms, through this next Season as they worked to get all her sisters married in good situations? And as she herself found a good situation?

He really didn't like Smallwood. But would he like any man?

As he watched Smallwood's tenderness with her, the intensity on his face, a small twinge of guilt bothered him. Was he standing in the way of Miss Standish's choice for happiness?

No, he refused to believe it—at least, not yet. But he knew no one, not one person in all of the *ton,* would be good enough for her. Not even him.

Chapter Eleven

Lord Smallwood's small smile endeared her further to him. "Must he watch?" The sudden insecurity there charmed her.

"I'm not sure why, but I do believe he feels he must."

"He is not your guardian."

"I know."

"I should like to send a carriage for the ball at the pavilion."

She hesitated. Lord Smallwood's eyes were kind, but there was a calculating glint there which made her nervous. "I'm certain Lord Morley will lend us the use of his, but thank you. I look forward to our set."

He dipped his head. "Until then."

"Yes, thank you."

He turned and stepped down their front stairs. His carriage pulled up in front of Lord Morley's. It was a deep black with a beautiful gold crest. She would be in good hands were she to marry Lord Smallwood, were he to be sincere and ask for her hand.

She watched while he drove away.

"Does he make you happy?" Lord Morley's voice behind her made her jump.

She placed a hand at her chest and controlled her breathing. "Why must you sneak up on me?" She spun. "And where is—oh, you have it." She reached for the chest. "This is most exciting. Come. We must gather the sisters."

For some reason, she felt it important Lord Morley be present. As she passed a servant, she stopped the footman. "Please send word to the sisters to meet in the family drawing room."

They hurried to the comfortable room by the fire, and she opened the draperies as far as they would go.

Sunlight poured in. "Come, let's sit here in the light." She took a seat on a low-lying settee, and he joined at her side.

They both peered at the box. He leaned closer, close enough she could feel the space between them warm. A rich smell of spices, of earth, the sky, wafted in the air around them.

"You smell nice."

She laughed. "I was thinking the same of you."

She lifted her chin, their faces closer than usual. "Thank you." Her voice sounded soft to her ears, almost accepting of his presence. Perhaps she could forgive him. He'd shown a measure of restraint where Lord Smallwood was concerned, and had included her in the castle renovation discussion. She held up the box.

"How can we open it?"

"May I?" He reached a hand for it. "I believe this lock is old enough we could break it, if that's what you want to do."

Her sisters hurried into the room. "What has happened?" Charity hurried to her side.

"Nothing at all." She smiled. "Except the mason has found this box, hidden within the walls."

"Oh, that's incredible." Charity squeezed herself on the sofa at June's other side, pushing her closer to Lord Morley. She laughed as her whole body tipped, and she lost her balance into him.

He lifted the box up so it was protected and offered his shoulder as a shield. "Whoa, there."

"Sisters, look at this. Should we call the mason to come break the lock for us?"

"Someone who lived here hid it in the wall?" Charity seemed equal parts hopeful and disbelieving.

"It seems so. We won't know anything about it until it's opened."

Grace kneeled at June's feet. "Then what are we waiting for? Let's do it."

Lord Morley lifted his eyes toward the doorway, where, in most houses, a servant always stood. "You need more servants."

"We have many more than we've ever had. I asked some to not hover about too closely."

"Why would you do that when I expressly asked them to hover?" Her eyebrow lifted, and he pressed his lips together. "But all as you wish, of course," he added. "I know it is not for me to say."

"Thank you."

"But have you considered your safety? The wall has just barely completed. Until then, anyone could have come upon you."

"Not really, and yes, servants were stationed there and at the front door. We really are quite safe. In part, thanks to you."

He seemed pacified.

Grace stood. "Oh, heavens. I shall summon a servant."

Within a few minutes, Mr. Smithson arrived with a rock and hammer. "You're certain you wish for me to go smashing things?"

"Yes, we wish to see what's inside."

"I thought you might. If everyone can back away just a little." He rested the hanging lock on the rock he'd brought and in one blow had the metal crushed and falling to the floor.

Grace lifted the box and carried it carefully back to June's lap. Everyone gathered around.

Lord Morley smiled.

"What? This is so exciting, isn't it?" June's hands cradled the package.

"It is, but my smile comes more from all you ladies gathered around me like this. I feel as though I have a new family of long-lost sisters."

Miss Standish searched his face. Did he really have no romantic sensibilities toward her? Was this all out of duty?

Then his gaze met hers, and the depth, the spark, the earnestness she saw said nothing of brotherly affection.

She looked away. Nothing about her feelings for Lord Morley was simple.

Then she placed her hands on the sides of the chest on her lap as though it was made for a lady to hold. "Are you ready?"

They giggled.

As she lifted the lid, everyone gathered closer, and she herself was full of those same feelings of family, mixed with an almost distracting sensation of warmth and expectation coming from Lord Morley. His side, pressed against hers, his earthy smell, his smile and care, were almost too much for her to resist.

And resist she must.

Inside the box were pouches—the kind typically used for jewelry—and a piece of leather, folded, closed with a seal.

"It's Father's seal."

Lord Morley looked closer. "What seal is this?"

"It's his family seal. The Normans."

"And not the Northumbers who came to own this castle? Your cousins?"

"Right. My grandfather was descended from the other brother, the son who wasn't the heir. He was also the most trusted general of the Molyneaux family. He had his own titles and estates. This was their seal."

She lifted the leather and handed it to Lord Morley. The seal was of two lions. "Perhaps from the earliest Normans?"

"I think so."

"Do you still have the ring?"

She nodded. "Yes, it's among their things. In my room."

He nodded, his expression curious. What more did he know about this branch of their family?

She reached for the bags. They were so fragile, the first fell apart in her hand. She gasped and peered into the chest. A necklace had fallen, and a bright red stone twinkled back at her. "A ruby?"

"Yes, it appears so." Lord Morley grinned.

She carefully pulled out other pouches and separated out jewels in each one. Deep blues, the clear of diamonds, and more rubies sparkled back. The last two waited. Kate reached in a shaky hand. "May I just hold it?" She lifted the rubies up to the light. "These are splendid. Have you ever seen anything so lovely?"

"No, of course I haven't." June lifted the last bag. It seemed sturdier than the rest and felt heavy. Inside were coins. She poured some out in her hand. "Gold coins." She studied a piece. "The Duke of Normandy?" She handed a piece to Lord Morley.

"This is rare indeed." He lifted the leather. "Shall we read this?"

"I hate to break the seal."

"Why? Break it. For goodness sake, do you not wish to see what's written there?" Charity crossed her arms. "I would have gone there first."

Lord Morley laughed, and June appreciated he enjoyed Charity's humor.

"Let's break it, then." She lifted the leather, and slid her finger under the seal. Then she unfolded what seemed to be a very old communication.

"Read it aloud. Oh, read it, June." Lucy danced in front of them all, her usual careful composure totally lost.

June nodded, swallowing. "I, William, Duke of Normandy..." her hands shook. "It is from his hand." She looked at them all. What did this mean?

"Read it!" Charity leaned forward as if she might take it.

"I will. Right:

I, WILLIAM, DUKE OF NORMANDY, DO HEREBY BEQUEATH THIS land and castle to the Molyneux family, my most loyal general, to his descendants from this time and forever. The jewels in this chest are gifts for his daughters and their daughters and so on, through time. May you care for this bequeathal and keep it for generations to come."

HER HANDS SHOOK. "SIGNED BY KING WILLIAM HIMSELF." She ran her finger along the lettering. "And here below are some markings. It looks like generations of his family." She peered closer, holding up the old leather. "I see our Molyneaux line. I see the general. He was...William's brother?"

Lord Morley looked over her shoulder. She felt his soft breath on her shoulder, which sent tingles down her arm.

She lifted a set of deep, blue stones and fingered their smooth texture. "I've never seen anything so amazing." She turned to Lord Morley. "Do you suppose our great-grandmother or great-great-grandmother wore these?"

He nodded. "I can only imagine they did. But surely others would have worn them after. Why were they hiding in this chest?"

Charity nodded. "I would like to know as well. Do we know our history? Why the family is so dispersed and almost hidden from each other? Where is the rest of the Molyneux line now?"

"That is an excellent question, isn't it?" Lord Morley's eyes shone. "I'm looking at five of them now. At least we know that."

"And Great Uncle. He must have been a Molyneux."

"Perhaps. But who did he pass this estate on to, leaving you as tenants?"

"A cousin originally, who left it to the duke, who gambled it away to you." She turned hurt eyes up to Lord Morley's and was comforted somewhat by the obvious understanding in his gaze.

"I'm sorry."

"And now I suppose these jewels, these coins—even this priceless letter from our great forebearer—all belong to you?"

He opened his mouth and then closed it. "I—I don't know."

Kate had placed the necklace around her throat. But now she turned to him. "Should we at least hide them with him for safe-keeping?"

"Oh, no." He held up his hands. "I'm staying at an inn. How about I investigate this situation further? Until then, hide these with Miss Standish's things, perhaps with your father's ring, until we know for certain."

"Might I wear it a little longer?" Kate's hand went up to her neck.

"The clasp might break." June shook her head. "Though you do look lovely in rubies."

"One thing we can do is have them all reset at a jeweler in London." Lord Morley said. "Or sell them."

"No." All the sisters responded at once.

Lord Morley nodded.

"Though, as they are likely yours, you may do as you wish." June hated the bitter taste in her mouth at even the mention of his ownership. She'd never felt so connected, so acknowledged as part of the royal line, as she did in this moment. Somehow the voice of William the Conqueror called to her, as if his hand was reaching out. And she felt a part of something—like she belonged.

She turned to Lord Morley. "Then what happened? To the Normans? To this castle?"

"I'm not certain. After the Norman takeover, there was a later war. The Normans were divided, and the French became French and the English stayed English. I'm not certain how your family fared in the division. That was in 1200 or so. And we will have to check our history books to discover the rest." He clasped her hand. "But this is exciting. You are truly from one of the noblest, oldest families in England."

Her shoulder lifted in a half shrug. "I care more that I know them than that they are revered. Being revered has only blessed me so far in this life. It has provided a barely subsisting level of life up until knowing you and the Duke."

"I understand."

"I like the revered part." Kate swirled in her dress. "I doubt the Duchess of York would have gifted me this gown if I had come from a line of peasants." She swirled some more and danced about the room.

June leaned back in her sofa and fell into the crook of Lord Morley's arm, the sensation so much like an embrace she almost snuggled up against him. Then she started and jerked herself upright. "This is all so new in some ways and yet so much of the same of what we have always known."

"What is new?"

Lucy sat across from them. "We have our own personal letter and jewels from a conquering king of England. The most famous Norman who ever lived."

"And what have you always known?"

"It doesn't matter one whit we are related to such a man." June held her hands out. "But you've done well by us. You've helped us live here, comfortably, in our ancestral home—something I didn't think would ever be possible otherwise. I could be happy here for all my days." She felt her tears well, and she didn't even care. "Especially after seeing the stone, running my fingers on those walls, considering the new and the old. It's moving and important."

Lord Morley placed his large, warm hand over hers, and the gesture felt nice, comforting. It made her want to lean back again and feel enveloped in his physical presence, but she resisted.

Instead she looked to her sisters. "What say you? You're all so quiet."

"I'm so happy. Rubies!" Kate spun on the other side of the room.

"Quiet, except for Kate." June laughed.

Charity, who had moved to stand by the fire, returned. "I think there is much more to be learned of our history. And my fingers itch with the desire to turn those pages."

"I'm not certain where to access such histories."

"Nor am I, but perhaps Gerald knows. The Duke of Granbury. He is named after his early ancestor, Fitzgerald, an English name adapted from the Normans. You are a relation of his, are you not?"

"I think so. He said he was informed of his new ownership by a letter from his cousin."

Lord Morley nodded. "He will be arriving any day."

Lucy seemed to be deep in thought.

"And you, Lucy? What say you?"

"I think this aids considerably in my quest for a title. To give back to our family name, bring back those of title."

"And because you're personally fascinated with the prospect." Charity crossed her arms.

"Yes, and that. But I see no harm in it. One of us is going to have to marry well."

"One of you? All of you." Lord Morley nodded. "In fact, I have just received a correspondence from the duke himself. He has agreed to increase your dowries. Five thousand apiece."

The girls gasped, and June felt the air leave her. "What did you say?"

"He is a good man and is determined to do right by you. He hopes the added money will perhaps alleviate some of the embarrassment caused by his card game?"

"I'm certain it shall." June's world spun. "This changes so much for us. Now I am even more determined you shall all marry for happiness." She looked from face to face, her own happiness growing as she considered her sisters would have every opportunity.

"And Grace? You are unaccountably quiet."

Her hands were clasped in her lap, and she sat very, very still. After a moment, her lip quivered.

Charity immediately moved to share her chair and put her arm around her shoulders. "And what is this?"

"Oh." She waved her hand. "This is nothing." When a few more tears fell into her lap, she shook her head. "No, it's not nothing. You are all talking of marriage as though it is the best thing, what we all want, but if you go and marry someone titled or wealthy, won't you have to go live in their house? Manage their estate? What of the castle? What of us? What of our family?" She dropped her face into her hands, and the sisters were silent in response.

June didn't know what to tell her except for one thing. "I don't imagine I'll be leaving. I shall stick to my happy rooms upstairs and read and play the harp. You may stay or visit as often as you wish."

Lord Morley looked as though he wanted to say more in response to June's comment, but he turned to Grace. "You can all visit. I shall leave the castle open to you whenever you should require it." Lord Morley looked as though his offer would be magnanimous, but upon exiting his lips, it felt to June more like false help, or perhaps a rub of salt in the wound, at any rate—not the comforting message he assuredly hoped to portray. For could he not see the castle always felt like theirs? Something about this found chest in the walls proved it to June. But she knew legally it could not be so. She had better grow accustomed all over again to the fact her life was owned by another.

Chapter Twelve

The days approached to the start of the prince's ball at his palace in Brighton, and hopefully before the event, Gerald would arrive.

Lord Morley stayed away from the sisters for two days and felt like all was lost and lonely in his world. He had to get back to London, to society, to his own study—something to help him remember who he was before he had become the leaseholder for a group of women.

He amended even his thoughts: not just any group of women —the Standish sisters. They were dear, as dear as any sisters could be. And the mystery of their family, their ancestry, intrigued him more than any other. He'd sent off correspondence to see if anyone knew the details, and he'd sent an express telling Gerald to bring his paperwork.

No matter what they discovered, he'd fallen in love with the castle and was quite pleased with the progress made to recover it.

Today he had convinced the sisters to join a group in a picnic at the beach. Lady Annabelle informed him of it and wished him to go, which he insisted was only possible if the Standish sisters joined. She'd grumbled about even numbers and then had extended an invitation to a greater amount of men to make do.

It had been a full week since the assembly, and today he planned to start spreading the word of their dowries. But he was loathe to do so. Perhaps he could pick and choose their matches before letting others know. For though the dowries were not the largest he'd ever heard of, they were substantial enough that, added to the notoriety of their family name, they were a good match to any man.

At least he thought so.

Their carriage arrived at the beach side.

"Oh, how lovely!" Lucy's starry eyes were directed toward a large group of men in breeches and top hats.

He laughed. "What is lovely?"

Her face colored, and she stepped down from the carriage. "Why, the water, of course."

"Of course," he murmured. "I think, or at least it is rumored, that Lord Stratton, the duke's son, will be coming to the prince's ball."

She sucked in a breath.

"In the meantime, there are many men of title right here." He pointed out several.

She nodded and lifted her chin. "Thank you."

He dipped his head. "And Grace, how pleased are you to be joining us?"

She clapped her hands. "As pleased as I ever was." She hurried forward onto the tiny rocks that made up the Brighton beach.

Charity had handed herself down in the moment when he'd been talking to Grace, but Kate awaited his hand. "They're all so lovely. Do you think my dress is appropriate?"

"To run about on the beach in the wind and water? Most certainly." Charity grinned, shaking her somewhat faded skirts.

"I hope so." Kate's worried expression caused Morley to dip his head closer.

"You look beautiful," he said.

"Oh, thank you."

He turned. "And now for the loveliest Standish." He held out a hand, quite enjoying her bright yellow morning dress and her matching bonnet. "You are like the sun today, Miss Standish, except I dare not look away." He bowed and reached for her hand.

"You are all compliments this morning." Her small smile, always demure, was warm. And a bright pink on her cheeks told him she was not unaffected by his compliments.

Energy coursed through him, the very happiness at escorting them added an extra lift to his step. "It has been two days without the sight of you all, and I find my heart brimming with warm solicitude."

"And so well spoken." She giggled, and he found the sound so musical he wished to hear it again.

"And why should I not be?"

"No reason at all. It suits you."

He tucked the hand she'd given him into the crook of his arm. "And now shall we explore the wilds of the beach? And meet these lovely picnickers as well?"

"Yes! Oh, yes, please." Grace began walking ahead.

"Wait for us, dear, of course."

She paused, but only for a moment.

"You don't have to wait for them, Grace. I'm here." Charity linked her arm and they hurried forward.

Kate and Lucy linked arms, and for a moment Morley breathed deeply in satisfaction, for all seemed right in the world.

"Miss Standish." Smallwood's voice, like a rancid disease, crept its way over to them.

He groaned. "Are we not rid of him?"

"Rid of him? I thought he was in the realm of acceptable, except for your personal and pointed dislike."

"My personal and pointed dislike might be enough. Shall I have to look at his face at family dinners?"

Her smile grew, and her eyes lit with happiness. "Family dinners?"

Then he looked away. "I suppose at some point I will no longer be invited."

"You shall. You shall come and enjoy."

"For that, I thank you. Now that I know you all, I don't think I should be able to bear living in a world devoid of the Standish sisters." He felt so cheery at being thought of as family he almost had a welcoming greeting for Smallwood on his lips.

"I can take it from here, Morley." Smallwood held his arm out for Miss Standish to take.

"You may not." He placed a hand over hers.

But she wiggled her hand away and then waved at them both with her fingers. "I think I shall walk freely. I'd like to try my hand at balancing on these rocks without a strong arm to lean on. They feel so odd beneath one's slippers, do they not?"

Smallwood hurried to her side, but Morley let her be. As the two hurried on ahead—Smallwood making a fool of himself almost at her feet, chasing as she walked faster—Morley drank in the lovely sounds of the sea. The gentle, lazy, crashing of waves on the shore, a distant cry of gulls. It all seemed to wash over him and brought a sense of calm.

Then a new hand rested on his arm.

"I hoped you would be here," Lady Annabelle's voice purred.

Her voice disrupted the calm, but he nodded. "Lady Annabelle. Thank you for inviting us to this picnic. It looks to be the premiere event in Brighton."

Her eyes narrowed as she studied the group gathering under the large tent. "It does, doesn't it? There are some who would not deign to come, and of course it is rumored Prince George is already here at the Royal Pavilion. But we have a good group, plenty for your Standish friends to know."

"Thank you. Your assistance in this matter is most desperately needed."

"I'm pleased to help. They're lovely girls. And did I hear their dowries have all been established?" Her eyebrows shot higher on her forehead.

"They have. The Duke of Granbury wrote me this week, though how you've come upon the information, I'm not certain if I want to know."

"News of this sort travels quickly. You shall have no trouble finding suitors for them all, even the eldest, though she is almost on the shelf."

He bristled inside, but he kept his expression bland.

As they approached, the sisters were already fast in conversation with others and receiving introductions all around them. Morley was pleased, until the group around Miss Standish seemed to grow. Smallwood was pushed to the outer circle as more bowed at her front. Her laugh carried out over the pebble beach to Morley.

His unease grew. Smallwood didn't seem to capture her admiration, but any of these other gentlemen could. And once she was introduced at Prinny's ball, anything could happen.

Did he wish her every happiness? Naturally. But he wished her happiness began and ended with him, not at the hand of some other gentleman.

The other sisters seemed safe and well cared for. Even Grace. He smiled. Lord Weatherby had taken to throwing rocks into the sea with her at his side. Some others noticed and were making their way over. All in all, the event had every reason to be a positive one. If only he could convince his heart this was the case—even without Miss Standish at his side.

Lady Annabelle began talking all about Brighton and the Season. "Our Season may hold fewer choices, but they are some of the most preferable. And when many are tired of London and the air and the smells and the crowd, they come to Brighton to bathe and breathe. Everyone is in a far better state of mind."

"I imagine so." He took his turn to breathe deeply. "I enjoy this air so much I wish I spent every day here walking the water."

"How is that dreadful inn?"

"It is not so very dreadful."

"Not when you can dine with the Standish sisters?" Her expression showed no emotion, but her eyes were still calculating.

"I don't know what you are trying to discover, but they are a lovely family, and I am doing my duty by them."

"And enjoying yourself?"

He dipped his head. "And enjoying myself immensely."

"Very well." She stepped closer. "But once everyone is paired off and your duty is done, perhaps we could try again, you and I?"

Her question seemed to come out of the blue and took him very much by surprise. But before he was required to answer, a familiar voice called out from behind.

"And he's come at last." Morley grinned at Lady Annabelle.

They turned.

"You, there!" Gerald waved. Her Grace, Amelia, walked on his arm. Morley chuckled at the sight of them. A jollier married couple he had yet to see.

He lifted his arm. "You, there."

"Keep me in mind, Morley. I won't be around forever." Annabelle tipped her head.

"Thank you. I acknowledge the honor of what you offer."

Then Gerald was upon them. He clapped Morley on the shoulder. "And how's my lucky best friend?"

Morley bowed over Amelia's hand. "Good to see you."

"And you." Her smile lit her whole face, and the beach seemed brighter.

"And you, former friend. I am only surviving. And much relieved you and Her Grace have come." They stood side by side and made their way toward the tent. "I should disown you as a friend."

"One day you just might thank me."

"Perhaps, but not any time soon, I'm afraid." He indicated

the crowd of men around Miss Standish. "And do you think this is easy? To take a family of women out in society? I feel like the *ton*'s most auspicious matron."

Gerald dipped his head back and laughed. Amelia joined in behind him, arm in arm with Lady Annabelle.

"I'm glad you are amused, but I am desperate. You must assist me."

"I've come to do just that. Now, what's this? You've brought the youngest out in society?" His frown amused Morley.

"Not out in society, but simply out for a picnic on the beach with her sisters."

"And a few overly attentive lords, if my eyes do not deceive me."

Morley looked closer. "I see what you mean." He picked up his pace. "We will talk more on this later."

Gerald waved him on.

Weatherby was talking to Grace, their faces close. What possible enticement did the young Miss Grace have for Weatherby? Morley couldn't fathom what his motivation could be, but he would feel much more comfortable with Grace on his own arm.

"Miss Grace." He bowed to them both.

She jumped and put some distance between herself and Weatherby.

"The Duke of Granbury has arrived and asked after you." He held out his arm.

"Oh, I'm so happy to hear it." She curtsied to Weatherby and then took Morley's arm.

As Morley led the youngest Standish away, he glanced over his shoulder to catch the last of a possibly interested Weatherby.

"Shall we go eat our picnic?"

"Oh, yes, I'm famished." She skipped along at his side. "I was beginning to wonder if people ate at picnics or merely stood around."

"Let us hope they eat."

Miss Standish sat on a blanket with Smallwood. Charity was in an animated conversation, surrounded by men who were equal parts amused and passionate about whatever she was expressing. He'd never met a woman like Charity.

Kate was surrounded by women, and the group of them were chattering at high levels of energy, their skirts swishing about them. And Lucy—his eyes scanned the area for Lucy and then landed on her, at the duke's side, smiling quietly and conversing with Amelia.

He led Grace to a free blanket and went to retrieve her food. As he passed the duke, he indicated with his head, and his friend moved to join her. Some of Morley's concern lessened in that moment. Perhaps the duke would really assist and he would no longer be alone in his efforts.

Miss Standish's beautiful laugh hung like musical notes in the air around him. As he turned his head to follow the sound, her eyes met his, and he was captured, not daring to breathe until she looked away again. Then the world sped up, and he resumed his path to the food tables. Oh, he was lost. And he wasn't certain what to do about it.

Chapter Thirteen

June only half listened as Lord Smallwood went on about his latest horse purchase. She was interested in horses. At one point in her life, she'd dreamed of a large stable. And he was a handsome man, and attentive. But her gaze drifted over to Lord Morley and Lucy and Grace, sitting with the duke and duchess.

She was relieved Her Grace had come. Perhaps the presence of the duchess would take some of the odd, awkward feelings that disturbed her when Lord Morley was near. And perhaps she could confide in the woman. She seemed genuine, caring.

Lord Smallwood lifted her fingers into his hand. "I have been happier getting to know you this past week than I have been in a long time."

His eyes were earnest, his attention solely on her. He pressed his lips to the back of her glove. "Might I have permission to court you more seriously?"

They sat mostly alone. He spoke quietly. Though she was taken aback by his timing, she was not surprised he asked such a question.

"I—" She looked down, searching for the proper words to

use. "I am flattered by your request. Might I think about it for a day or two?"

"Certainly. I am not in a hurry...yet." He lowered her hand. "I'm looking forward to Prinny's ball. Perhaps you will know then?"

She nodded. "Yes, I will have an answer for you."

He then talked of the other couples, the people sharing their tent. "This whole event was planned in part for your benefit." He lifted a cup and indicated a pretty woman Lord Morley had spoken to earlier. "Lady Annabelle offered to assist Lord Morley in helping you and your sisters move forward in your social standing here in Brighton. So she included you on the invitation list and then invited more of the local gentlemen to round out the numbers."

"And what is she to Lord Morley?"

Lady Annabelle had slinked over closer to Lord Morley and her sisters until the duke noticed her and invited her to join them. She sat as close as it seemed possible to Lord Morley, leaning across him somewhat as she greeted everyone else on the blanket.

June tried not to be bothered by a scene she didn't totally understand, but Lord Smallwood's words seemed to be proven by her view at that moment.

"They have a past. And perhaps a future? I think his mother approves, which is a remarkable feat in and of itself. Lady Morley is most adamant he marry well, and many a lady have not passed muster."

"How interesting. I know nothing of his family."

"Well, you wouldn't. He's a private sort of fellow about some things, Annabelle being one."

As June studied them, she saw some regard in his expression as he looked at her, some deference to her in conversation. They seemed familiar. Perhaps Lord Smallwood knew of what he spoke.

"Lord Morley is ruled by duty." Lord Smallwood's breath

tickled her neck. She knew if she turned, his face would be very close—too close—so she kept turned away.

"Hmm."

A great restlessness filled her, and more than anything, she wanted to stand and take a turn—or a run, more like. She eyed the shoreline and wished to skip through the shallow, foamy water.

Soon everyone was finishing up their food, and the servants were cleaning up. When Grace stood before her, standing by the duke and duchess, June could not have been more pleased.

"Come walk with us, June." Grace held out her hand.

"I should like that very much." She turned to Lord Smallwood. "You'll excuse me?"

"Or I could accompany?"

"I think my sister is seeking some sisterly counsel."

"Ah, which might not be so easily shared if I accompanied you?"

"Precisely. You understand."

He nodded and stood quickly, reaching a hand down to help her rise.

As soon as the three were out of earshot, Grace squeezed her arm. "We have the duchess all to ourselves."

To June's surprise, Her Grace giggled. Then she leaned across her sister so she might smile at June. "I have heard so much about the role you played in helping Gerald with the other sensitive situation. How can I ever thank you?" June had aided him in avoiding an entrapment to a woman who still lived nearby, the woman in question having eloped with a footman, of all things.

June felt her face heat. So much exuberance and gratitude focused on her was overwhelming. "I don't think any thanks are in order, really. We have been so blessed ourselves by the care of your husband." She waved a hand back to the picnic. "All of this is possible now. I can hardly believe it."

Grace sighed. "Yes, men are interested in us now."

June laughed. "Grace, it will be a few years yet for you."

"A few?" Her face drained of color. "But I thought surely I could have my Season next."

"You are still young, and our other sisters aren't married. You don't mind waiting?"

The growing pout on her lip showed she very much cared, but she said nothing more.

Then the duchess smiled a warm and caring smile. "Who is the man doting so much attention on you?"

"Oh, that is Lord Smallwood."

"And?" Her eyes danced with excitement.

"And...I don't know. He is attentive." She looked down and watched the pebbles as she walked. "There is a bit of news to share. Might I?" Her eyes sought the duchess's.

"If your question is will I keep your confidence, my answer is most definitely."

"I trust you will. My concern stems more from whether you care to be bothered with such trivial concerns so unrelated to yourself."

"On the contrary. I feel very involved and care deeply for your situation and happiness."

June studied her in wonder. "You are too good, too kind, the both of you."

"Morley as well. He's of the opinion you sisters are now his personal responsibility."

"Yes, I know." June looked away, not certain how to keep the disappointment out of her voice.

"But I do not believe he acts solely out of duty."

"Don't you?"

"No. His affections seem to have been captured."

"Your Grace—"

"Oh, call me Amelia, please. I need at least one friend who will address me as a friend and not as some creature to be revered."

"Might I call you Amelia as well?" Grace's hopeful expression told June just how much she longed for family, for friendship and familiarity with others.

"Of course. Your entire family may."

"I don't know if Lucy would." Grace frowned. "I think she prefers the titles."

"And that would be acceptable too."

June could feel her gaze. She had so many questions. What did she mean about Lord Morley's heart being captured? That he felt like one of the family? He'd said it often enough. June knew he had interests in knowing her better, but in what way? She couldn't always feel like a duty to him. Was he so dutiful he'd marry her himself if no one else asked?

Even if she told herself she was happy to spend her days in the castle with her books, even if she told Lord Morley such a thing, would he then ask for her, just to ensure they were all married?

Well, she wouldn't wait to find out.

June?" Amelia smiled. "You had news to share?"

"Oh, yes, I am woolgathering. Something you said is dancing around in my mind." She swallowed. "Lord Smallwood asked me just now if he might court me more seriously."

Grace gasped. "You can't allow him."

"What? Why not? Why does no one seem to approve of him? He's respectable in every way, handsome, and seems interested in me." June turned away, exasperated.

"Who else doesn't approve?" Amelia's soft voice brought her attention back to the two of them.

"Lord Morley, I suppose. He's the only other one."

"And the others. Charity doesn't like him." Grace pointed out.

"That's just because he has Tory leanings." June shook her head.

Amelia laughed. "Oh, I like Charity, then."

"I can't understand what is so wrong with him. If someone such as him were to be doting on any of you, I'd be pleased." She felt her eyes burn. "I never thought I'd be the one with a match. I'd all but planned to be the one alone. And here someone very eligible is interested. Why should that be so wrong?" And the real issue, how could she turn away the only man to show real interest in her? Real, unmotivated by duty, honest to goodness, interest. She simply couldn't afford to turn that away.

"You told him you want to think about it? Why?"

"I wish to know for certain the leanings of my heart. I don't want to toy with a man's emotions. I felt it unfair."

"Absolutely. You are an honorable sort of person with a loving heart. Any of these men in the *ton* would be happy for the rest of their days to have a woman such as you at his side."

June's heart swelled. "I hear you. But I find your words floating in the air above me. Not one of them is sinking in." She shrugged. "As much as I would like them to." She looked out over the water. "After all this time of feeling like we were just the wealthy class castoffs, women to be pitied and helped because of our fall, I wonder if there are people left who might value us for other things, see the worth of our hearts, our humor, our minds, the things you mentioned—our honor." Oh, it felt so freeing to share her feelings.

Grace squeezed her arm. "I didn't know you felt this way."

"I don't suppose anyone did. But I did. I do. And I just don't see how finding a bit of my own happiness would be wrong."

"Oh, dear June. Might I call you June?"

"Certainly. I'd like that."

"More than anything, I'd like for you to be happy. Perhaps the others just haven't seen anything in Lord Smallwood they think would make you happy. If it's there, if he is the one who makes your heart sing, then let the others see it. Let them see what is special about this man."

And now June's passion about the subject of her happiness fizzled. For she knew Lord Smallwood didn't really make her happy. But he was the first to have any potential to do so, and she didn't want to throw that away either. Happiness was a precious commodity in her situation. "Thank you. I'll do my best."

"And now for the other subject that had your mind turning?" Amelia's mouth lifted at the corner, and June suspected her capable of a great many subterfuges.

Before June could say anything, Grace piped up. "I'll say what I was thinking. I think you should give Lord Morley a chance. He's perfect. He's like a big brother already, and I wouldn't like to lose him."

"So I should marry him so you can keep him as a brother?"

"And if you love him. I thought you did care for him, for a moment." Grace searched her face, and the innocence in Grace's features opened her mouth to words she was not planning on sharing.

"He's perfectly wonderful," June said. "We all know it. But I don't like being beholden to him. Out of duty, he'd marry us all if he could."

Amelia snorted, and June quite loved her all the more for the perfectly unladylike noise. "You think so? You think Morley capable of such a dishonesty?"

"Dishonesty? No. I'd never consider him anything but perfectly upright."

"Then why would he be capable of marrying for duty only when he would be pledging to love, honor, and cherish?"

June hadn't considered marriage to be much more than a business arrangement, one she hoped her heart would be engaged in. But as Amelia spoke, she wondered if perhaps in the world there were still people who considered their marriage promises to be real, who desired to love their wife.

"He'd never pretend. You are correct." At those words, her heart let go of the pinching cage around it. Perhaps if he was interested in pursuing more with her, he'd express his wishes, and he'd tell her exactly what he hoped from her. And she knew when he did, she could trust his words. Or at least, she sincerely hoped she could. "If Morley is not trustworthy, there is not a man in England who is."

"I know Gerald would trust him with his life—has, on occasion." Amelia smiled such a soft and tender smile, June could see her love for Gerald.

"I am happy you and the duke found each other."

"I feel like miracles brought us together. Many. And one of them was named Morley. He was an angel to us." She placed a hand on June's arm. "And you were another. June, I count you as a very special angel." They stopped walking. "We had the servants drop our things at the castle. Would you mind if we stayed in your fascinating home?"

"We would be honored." She took Amelia's outstretched hands in her own and looked into the eyes of sincere friendship.

Then Grace put her hands on her hips. "Are we still walking? Or just standing here? Or what are we doing? Because I wouldn't mind getting back."

June turned to the tent. Many of the others were leaving. The servants were cleaning, and soon the tent itself would be dismantled. "Oh, goodness. We can head back if you like." She squeezed Amelia's hands one more time. "Thank you."

"I don't know what for, but I am so happy to have finally met you."

"And I as well."

They changed direction and worked their way back up to the road where the carriages were arriving.

"Join me in our carriage," Amelia said.

"We'd love to."

Grace leaned in another direction. "Might I leave with Charity? I want to hear what she talked about for two hours surrounded by all those lords. She had the whole lot of them completely captivated."

June laughed. "Of course. And I suspect we shall hear everyone's stories by the fire with our chocolate."

Amelia clapped her hands. "Excellent, for I would so enjoy being a part."

They made their way to the grand ducal carriage. It had gold-gilded edges and a gorgeous crest, all in gold, on the side. The navy exterior shone in the sun. A footman opened the door, and June found a seat in the plush interior.

Would she ever live in such comfort? She ran her hand along the interior wood, where not a scratch marred the surface. She might. But she didn't need anything so fine. What she needed was love. Could she find that love in Lord Morley?

She closed her eyes, a smile tugging her lips as she allowed her thoughts to move in that direction.

"I'd love to know what delicious moments are passing through your mind to bring such a soft smile to your face."

Lord Morley's voice startled her in the best manner, but she couldn't possibly explain. "I'm not certain to what you are referring." She looked away. The duke and duchess joined them. And as the carriage began moving, the same smile began to grow.

"Hello, dear Miss Standish." The duke held his hand out to her. "Have I properly thanked you for the role you played in saving me from a very destitute life?"

"I think I have been completely and thoroughly thanked, Your Grace."

"Call me Gerald."

Stunned at the incredible familiarity, she swallowed twice before saying, "I couldn't."

Lord Morley laughed. "You could, once you know him better."

"Oh, never mind Morley. He's just still sore at me for the trick I played on him. But did I not choose well?"

"I'm confused." June looked from face to face and saw such a mixture of discomfort and humor, she wasn't certain she wanted to fully understand.

"I plan to tell all when we arrive back at the castle."

Chapter Fourteen

Morley sat across from Miss Standish in the carriage
with his best friend and his best friend's wife, and
he didn't think life could get any better. "I am
hoping when Gerald tells the story, perhaps you might forgive
me easier."

"Oh, there's nothing to forgive. You've been nothing but
gracious and kind and giving."

"And you might never be able to see me the same again
because of it." He searched her face.

Her gaze flitted to the duke and back to him twice before he
realized this conversation might be better expressed when not in
the company of others.

They arrived at the castle, and the chatter just inside the
doors told them they'd been beat by the other sisters, but only
just. Charity was saying something with great emphasis, using
her arms in great dramatic motions. Morley smiled.

"She must temper her conversation if she is ever to marry,"
June sighed.

Morley turned from Charity to June and back. "No." He
shook his head. "Perhaps I am biased, but she should stay just

the way she is. Somewhere out there is a chap confident enough to marry her."

Miss Standish's eyes widened, and then her lip quivered for just a second before she turned away.

It took every ounce of restraint not to pull her into his arms. Was she crying? Had he said something objectionable?

When she turned back with misty eyes, her warm and tender smile rewarded him. "I feel the same. It is what I wish for her, not daring to believe it could happen. Do you think we really could hope for such a thing? Hope she could find happiness in marriage?"

"Certainly. I don't see why not."

She placed a hand on his arm. "You are everything that is amiable and good. I don't know how it is you were dragged into our sorry lives, but I am pleased. So pleased." Her gaze lifted to meet his eyes, and then she looked away.

He placed his hand atop hers, and Gerald stood beside him, Amelia on his arm. "Let us convene in your lovely room for a moment before Amelia must rest."

"I'm perfectly healthy."

The old, familiar worry crossed Gerald's face when Amelia wasn't looking, and Morley knew that although he hid as much of it as he could, Gerald was plagued with concern his new wife would meet the same fate as his first. Childbirth had become less joy and more terror for his best friend.

Morley rested a hand on his shoulder. Gerald nodded, then pasted his pleasant smile back on and waved them toward the sitting room.

As soon as everyone gathered, with the duchess closest to the fire and a blanket wrapped around her, Gerald stood in front of them all with a flair.

"Perhaps you have wondered why we are all gathered here together this fine evening?"

"We know, Gerald. Perhaps we could make this less dramatic and more...to the point?"

"Certainly." But he continued on with his own flair anyway. "Perhaps you are considering why a man such as I, who proclaimed to care for you ladies, who in fact owes you a great debt—why I would do such a callous thing as toss your family estates onto a gaming table?"

Lucy gasped. "Is that what you did?" She placed a hand over her mouth. "Forgive me, but I had no idea. I mean, the others mentioned it at the assembly, but I couldn't believe it."

June laughed. "Where have you been, sweet?" She had kept her hand on Morley's arm even after they sat together on the sofa, and the lovely rushing sensations that moved up and down his arm raced with the hope that perhaps she was more inclined toward him and accepting of his attention.

Gerald placed a hand on his heart. "I did do that, with the full knowledge Morley here would win."

"But why would you want to be rid of us?" Grace's pout threatened to show itself, and Morley saw yet another evidence she was unprepared for the workings of the Season and the people she would meet during it.

"I did not want to be rid of you. On the contrary, I wished to be ever closer to you. For I did not toss you aside to some straggler. No, Morley is my best friend. He's more family than my actual family. And furthermore, I knew he would be more attentive than I am." He flicked his hand.

"So, was the duke our guardian? Is Lord Morley our guardian?" Grace's wrinkled forehead, as she looked from June to Morley and back, made him smile.

"I am not your guardian, no." Morley in many ways wished he were. But in some key ways, he was glad he was not.

She began to nod but then stopped. "But why are you here and helping us and hoping we marry?"

"Because he wants us out of his hair—and his castle." Charity crossed her arms with a look of challenge.

"Charity, really." June shook her head.

"No, June. Let him respond. The duke did the same. We are five burdens, no matter how you look at it."

June shrunk beside him, and her hand started to slide away from his elbow.

"Now, Miss Charity, Miss Standish—all of you lovely sisters. In some regards, what you say is true," Morley said.

All of them looked away, and Gerald frowned.

"I would like you out of this castle, if that is what you desire, married and happy on estates of your own," Morley went on.

Charity's frown continued.

"But I do not have hopes for the castle as my own place of residence in any way that would preclude any number of you staying here as well. This is your home for as long as you wish it to be so."

Charity seemed partly mollified, and June kept her hand on his arm. But the mood in the room had changed, and he longed for it to return to the lovely, cozy warmth he'd felt only moments before.

"And Gerald, tell them the good news," Morley said.

Gerald considered Morley for a moment, and then his face lit. "Ah, yes. Since I heard you may have been adversely affected by the knowledge your estates had been passed away at a game of cards, we"—Gerald shared such a look of love with Amelia that Morley felt almost indecent to witness the specialness between them—"we have decided you each deserve a larger dowry."

"Can it be?" Lucy stood, clasped her hands together, and then sat. Her cheeks flushed in pleasure.

"We have already set aside the money. And I hope the mending of the castle and a modest dowry, coupled with your impeccable family line, should be all you need in life to find a good partner in marriage."

"And a Season in London?" Lucy lifted her eyes in such hope Morley had to root for her in some ways.

"Perhaps." Morley nodded. "Perhaps. I do think everyone

visits here, so in most regards you are in the best position to meet whoever you like, honestly. In London, the invitations are limited. Though we could possibly attend any party we would like with His Grace's and my connections, I don't know if the invitations would include all five of you."

Lucy nodded. "I shall not give up hope."

"Very good."

The conversation continued, and Morley sat back, enjoying the close presence of Miss Standish on his arm. The sisters laughed and teased with Gerald. Amelia smiled and seemed most happy here with this group—much more so than with some of the suspicious and spiteful members of the *ton*.

Morley leaned closer to Miss Standish, enjoying the soft waft of rose that always hovered about her. "Thank you for this."

She lifted her eyes up to his. Her heart-shaped face, the soft pink to her cheeks, the round pools of the eyes that slowly blinked with questions and the light of expectation—it was all he could do to stop himself from pressing his lips to her forehead first, and then her cheek, then finding his way down to the soft, full lips.

She parted her mouth and wet her bottom lip. Then she cleared her throat. "Thank you? For...what?"

"For this friendship, for family. Everyone gathered here in this room has become dear to me."

Her expression clouded, and he wanted to kick himself for not being more clear. But the moment passed, and then Gerald rose from his seat, holding a hand out to his wife.

"We must retire."

Everyone stood and curtsied or bowed.

"Sisters, we should find our own beds." June had not yet removed her hand from his arm, even though now would be a natural time to do so, and he allowed her simple continuance of attention at his side to spur him on and give him courage.

"I will see you lovely sisters at the prince's ball, if not before.

I must admit, I'm more excited to see a bunch of gowns than I have ever been."

"Oh, our gowns!" Kate grinned and then linked arms with Grace as they made their way out of the room. Lucy and Charity followed, but not without Lucy checking over her shoulder twice and Charity dragging her from the room.

Morley walked with Miss Standish over closer to the fire. "I wonder if I might..."

She turned to him, "Yes?"

The bright eyes were his undoing. All coherent thought fled as he studied the flecks of blue amidst the green.

He leaned closer, and she took a step toward him. The candles and firelight visually filtering through her hair created a halo all around her head. He brought her hand up to his mouth and pressed his lips, lingering as long as he dared.

She closed her eyes, and he knew he couldn't wait until the ball to see her again. And he didn't want to always be surrounded by the others. This moment alone with Miss Standish might be his most enjoyable since arriving in Brighton, short though it was.

"Would you like to go to the theater with me?" he said.

Her eyes opened, and her mouth lifted in a delighted smile. "I would like nothing more."

He nodded. "I shall come tomorrow to fetch you. Gerald and Amelia can join us."

"Oh." Her cheeks colored. "And not the others?"

"They are more than welcome, but I thought, perhaps... perhaps there might be times when we could be together?" He held his breath. Never had he been so unsure around a woman. Never had he pursued one—not really.

But she showed no hesitation with her response. "I'd like that. Thank you."

"Very good." Energy rushed through him. "I'm pleased to hear it. I shall secure us a box forthwith." He stepped away and bowed. "And now I must say good night."

She smiled, her quiet happiness lifting his own.

As he turned from the room, his last view of her standing at the fire made him wish he never had to leave her in the evenings again. But in order for that to happen, she would have to see him in a completely different light. Did she, after this evening? After Gerald's explanation? Perhaps.

He had work to do, and a whole slew of sisters to marry off to worthy suitors—and to somehow keep away the ones vying for Miss Standish's attention. Not an easy task. Not any of it.

Chapter Fifteen

June danced back to her room, spinning and tipping her arms down and back up, her head full of happiness and dreams. As she tripped down the hall, she couldn't help the smile that stretched across her face. Could it be possible? Was Lord Morley interested in her, not out of obligation, but as a person? Did he prefer her to all others?

She skipped into her room and almost stumbled when she saw each of her sisters on her bed.

"What's this?" She smiled, but they seemed concerned. "Are you not well? Have we not had the best news? Dowries for each of you?"

Charity nodded. "Yes, that's all wonderful, but what about you? What are you doing with Lord Morley?"

"Charity." Grace pointed. "I don't know why you are so concerned. He likes her, doesn't he? Can't you tell they're in love?"

"Wait, I'm not—"

"In love? Him? Really?" said Charity. "Because I thought I saw a lot of attention given to a Lady Annabelle at the picnic. And I saw our June sitting with Lord Smallwood." Charity crossed her arms. "And good riddance to that one, but spending quiet moments by firelight when it's just us is one thing. Does he honor you with his attention when others are present?"

"Of course he does." June nodded. She had been the one to push him away. "But you are correct. If I wish to entertain attention from Lord Morley, I cannot be encouraging Lord Smallwood."

"I, for one, am thrilled to even be listening to this conversation." Lucy smiled. "Who would have thought even four months ago our June would be conversing about the merits of giving attention to one earl over another?"

"True." Kate leaned back against the headboard on June's bed. "And they are both as handsome as any man."

"Charity, is your concern his affection is not truly engaged—that he is toying with me?"

"My concern is you will be hurt. What do we know of his family, his obligations elsewhere? I've heard his mother is choosy with regard to him."

June frowned. "Lord Smallwood said something similar." She allowed Charity's concern to wash over her. "You are wise to warn me. But I see no harm in allowing his attentions. How will either of us know anything about the other if we don't move forward at least somewhat?"

Charity shook her head. "Must we all marry? I might be perfectly happy here in the castle, and I thought you might be planning the same."

She moved to sit by her next-youngest sister. "Ah, Charity. I had not thought any attention would be given me. I'd thought we would need to focus on the most likely of us all—you younger sisters—but now that opportunities present themselves, I should like to explore them. I don't aspire to be lonely."

"You wouldn't be. We'd be together. Why do any of us grow up? Do we not have all we need right here on this bed?"

The girls smiled at each other, and when June held out her arms, they crowded in together in one large hug.

"I shan't ever lose a single one of you." June squeezed harder. "No matter what."

They talked and giggled and shared stories long into the night, until they had all fallen asleep in various degrees of discomfort on June's bed. But she lay awake for many hours yet. Had she found a match in Lord Morley? Was he truly as interested as he seemed? Only time would tell, she supposed. It was a great evidence he'd invited her to the theater. She smiled in the darkness. The theater. She'd longed to go for many years, and one of the gowns most recently gifted by the Duchess of Sussex would be perfect for the outing.

THE DEEP ROYAL BLUE OF THE VELVET MATERIAL ALMOST shimmered, it was so fine. She was lucky to be close to the same size as the tall and slender Duchess of Sussex. Her long white gloves shone against the deep blue, and she wore her hair piled high on her head.

Amelia had lent her the use of her lady's maid, and as June skipped down the stairs, she had not felt more excited in a very, very long time.

"Slow. Walk slowly so we can admire you." Amelia's mellow voice made June smile.

She looked up and stopped short. "Oh! I didn't know you were all here." The duke and duchess stood side by side, and Lord Morley stood at the base of the stairs. He reached out his hand.

And then June took her time. She stepped with the grace and elegance her governess had taught her. She remembered her own mother in gowns of similar finery. "Thank you, Mother," she whispered. Perhaps she heard. June liked to think so.

The image of Lord Morley standing and waiting for her brought much of her life in a beautiful, complete circle, and she began to see him as a part of it all. One foot moved in front of the other until she reached out to take his hand.

He cradled it in his own, then bowed deeply. "Miss Standish." His respect—almost reverence—touched her. He placed his lips to the back of her glove, and the impression left tingles racing up her arm. Then he tucked her hand at his side on his arm. He nodded to the others. "Shall we be off?"

June smiled. "I'm looking forward to this. I've never been."

"Then I am pleased we can share in your experience." Amelia looked radiant.

June didn't mention her condition, but she was beginning to see evidence the duchess was with child, and she hoped all was well with her.

At Lord Morley's nod, the footman opened the door to the ducal carriage and then Morley entered and sat at her side. Again the four of them were in a carriage together, and she felt a surprising comfort and familiarity. Of all the people she'd met, she liked these three most.

"Shall we amuse the ladies with tales of our youth?" The duke's eyes gleamed wickedly.

"I think they would be most amused with *your* tales."

"True. And someone must be the foil against your noble nature."

"Has Lord Morley always been noble?" June asked without thought, wanting more than anything to know more of Morley.

The duke considered his best friend for many moments, and then he nodded. "I believe so, yes."

"Now, that just cannot be true, by virtue of my humanity. No young tyke is noble." Morley's face colored, and June was even more charmed.

"I beg to differ, perhaps, as I very much believe that you were." The duke leaned back on his carriage seat with his arm around his wife, clearly enjoying the attention. "You'll have to imagine with me. Young Morley over there and myself."

"Was he always Morley?"

"Well, now, he wasn't. Too true. Not to the others. But to me, he's been Morley."

"And I called him 'duke.'" Lord Morley laughed. "It was our way of making light of the responsibilities that would befall us."

"Too true. To be fair, you called me Gerald a fair amount. Still do."

"To be fair, I do. Perhaps when 'Duke' seems out of reach."

"Always keeping me on my toes."

"Just when my own life has been disrupted by your games."

June cringed. Was he complaining of his responsibility for her and her sisters?

But he lifted her hand. "In some cases your interference has not disrupted my life—with regard to the lovely Miss Standish, for example. But in other cases, you have caused mischief, like the time you convinced me to stand up to our maths instructor at Eton."

"That was not only me." Gerald held up his hands, his smile belying any real remorse.

"But you are the only person I would have done such a thing for."

"I was failing. If someone didn't ask for a reprieve on our marks, I would have had to retake the whole class."

"Hmm. And I got the ruler for it."

"I was sorry for that." Gerald did look sorrowful as he shook his head. "But didn't I stay by your side the night through while it stung?"

"Yes, you did."

"And wasn't that the most noble of all things to do?"

June laughed. "It was certainly giving of you."

Amelia shook her head. "Morley stood up for me to the other members of the *ton* when no one else knew who I was."

Lord Morley nodded. "And that was easy to do, as deserving as you are and as unworthy as they can sometimes be."

"Well, I thank you for it now."

They pulled in front of the theater.

Morley peered out their carriage window. "It has just opened and promises to be stunning. The New-Road Theater."

June sucked in a breath. "Already I'm quite amazed." The structure rose up to great heights in front of them.

A footman opened the door, and as June stood on the arm of an earl, accompanied by a duke and duchess, she felt what it might be like to move in their circles.

Everyone looked their way. The most glittering and fashionable of the day had an eye for their arrival, and June felt acutely observed. But she smiled. Lord Morley kept her close as they walked through a large gathering of people in front of the theater. As soon as they stepped inside, the noise decreased, for which June was grateful. The building was lined with red—the carpeting, the walls, the ceilings, the curtains on the outside of boxes.

Gerald led them to a stairwell. Many looked as though they might want to talk to the duke or the earl or Amelia, but June's group kept walking. When at last they stepped inside a curtained box of six chairs, Lord Morley grinned.

"And now to watch the performance."

She sat beside him on the front row of their box. The duke sat at his other side and Amelia far down at the other end. The boxes across from theirs were filling. The women's dresses were beautiful. Some sparkled in the light. Their hair was done up on their heads, some to the greater heights she remembered on her mother when she was younger.

She leaned forward to look down. "Oh!" The bottom floor of the theater was filled with all manner of people, some fancily dressed, others not. But all seemed to ignite the house with energy.

Her eyes were drawn more often than not to Lord Morley beside her. His cravat was crisp and white, and she'd never given it much thought before, but she found the effect against his jawline enticing. She embarrassed herself into realizing she was imagining just how it would feel to run her hand along his face, at his jaw.

Lord Morley lifted his chin, obviously noting her attention. "It's called the Mathematical." He turned his head this way and that.

She tried to pretend it was the tie all along that held her attention. "How do you tie it?"

"Oh, my valet fashions it."

"You discussing your knot?" The duke laughed. "Amelia and I tried to tie one once. And let us just say it is good the experts take care of such things for us."

June laughed. The duke was a dear and so perfectly married to Amelia.

June felt eyes on her from outside their soft comfort. She looked across the way again and saw the cause: Lady Annabelle. She was laughing and smiling with the people in her box, but her eyes were set squarely on June and Lord Morley.

What was her interest there? She'd have to consider her later. Now was not the time to give Lady Annabelle one ounce more attention than June cared to give her.

Lord Morley moved his chair closer. "I heard if you watch the side of the stage, you will see a surprise entrance."

"Oh?" Her eyes trained on the spot. "Thank you."

"Tell me, Miss Standish—tell me of your parents."

Surprised, she nodded. "I miss them terribly."

"I imagine so. I miss my father." His face dropped, his lines more prominent.

Her heart went out to him so, without thinking, she placed a hand on his arm. "It is harder than I realized it would be to lose a parent, two parents. They were wonderful people. Father was the third son and happily cared for a parish of lovely people in the west of England."

"Ah. No wonder." His eyes sparkled at her in the darkness.

"No wonder what?"

"Your family is so full of goodness. You have been taught well."

"Hmm. We have, yes. Father's favorite sermons were straight out of Psalms. And I do believe I enjoyed those best."

"And your mother? Who looks like her most?"

June smiled. "I think Charity, with her red hair. But we all have a certain quality about us that is much like our mother. An air, more like."

"Interesting. I am certain she was beautiful."

June's heart skipped. Did he think her beautiful too? "She was. She practiced what Papa used to preach, as they say. Every Sunday we were about sharing and giving and loving. We visited more often than we sat." June laughed, remembering. "Which was fine with me. I didn't much like sitting."

"I feel like I know them better now. Thank you."

"And your parents? Are you more like your father or mother?"

"My father, most definitely."

"Tell me about him."

"He died too young. He was much older than my mother, but I feel his loss every day. He had more years to give, certainly. But he was suddenly taken ill, and I arrived only in time to say goodbye to his last few breaths."

"How terribly sad."

"Yes, it was. And we move on, for that is the way. I became an earl, and my mother became...worried."

"Oh? And why is she worried?"

"For her son," Gerald interrupted with a laugh. "She worries night and day about Morley here. And for no good reason. Does he look like he needs to be worried over?"

June laughed along. "Well, no. Unless one needs to worry he has taken it upon himself to marry off five women."

"That is something to worry about, to be sure." Lord Morley stretched against his cravat. "But things are looking up. We shall find suitors for each one of you lovely Standish sisters. Lords, even. Shall we find lords for the Sisters of Sussex?"

"Lucy would thank you."

"Lucy. That woman will marry a duke."

"Which one?" The duke huffed. "I don't know a single young duke."

"But the young Lord Fenwick." Lord Morley smiled. "He'll be a duke one day."

June couldn't help but feel disappointed he'd grouped her in conversation as one to be married off. Her earlier concerns he only viewed her as an obligation to fulfill resurfaced.

But Lord Morley lifted her hand. "I find my responsibility to help you in this regard most odious."

Her mouth dropped open, and she tried to pull her hand away. She began to stand. "Believe me, it is not my intent to be a burden—"

"No, please. I tease, or I mean to flatter." Lord Morley ran a hand through his hair, muffing it in all directions, looking so undeniably vulnerable she paused before what would have been a swift pace to the back of their box.

"I don't wish to be worried over," June said. "I wish for matches for my sisters and none else. I will spend my days happily in the castle alone."

"But is that what you truly wish? To be alone?"

"Of course not, but I don't wish to be a trouble, that is for certain."

"I wish to explain—please. What I meant was forcing myself to allow you to meet the men of the *ton*, to give them chances to woo you, watching them fawn over you and perhaps steal you from me—" He cleared his throat. "I find that odious."

Her breath caught. "Oh. I see." Her smile spread.

Before she could respond, the theater candles started to dim, and the curtains closed.

She was still as far as ever from understanding Lord Morley's intentions. But he'd convinced her of this much: she'd caught his eye. And she knew she wished to stay right where she was.

Chapter Sixteen

After the theater, Lord Morley dropped Miss Standish off at her home with the promise they and all the sisters could walk the South Downs. The white cliffs promised to be some of the most beautiful sights in all of Brighton. A group of them was going out for a walk, and the sisters had talked of it.

The ball was just a week away. Had he asked for two sets with Miss Standish? He couldn't remember. He'd thought of it often enough he could have forgotten to actually petition for the sets.

She entered her home on Amelia's arm. The two had kept up a constant dialogue about the actors, the parts they played, and what was to be loved or despised in each. Then the duke sent the carriage on to take Morley back to his inn. He was mighty tired of his separate accommodations, but he just did not feel comfortable sleeping in the castle. Now that Amelia and Gerald arrived, he could move in, but no one had asked him to.

As he climbed down from his carriage, the evening air felt chill. The Steine was active with people taking night strolls. The Royal Pavilion looked lit and full of magic; its bulbous round towers with spindles seemed otherworldly. The inn seemed dark and lonely. Instead of entering, he headed out on the great walkway which circled along the stores and in front of the Royal Pavilion. The sound of the waves crashed behind him. He picked up his pace to fight the chill.

As he made his way along the Steine toward the water, he nodded pleasantly to people he passed and considered Brighton as a whole. It was lovely, and it was an excellent place for the sisters to become married. If Brighton was any larger, he would not be able to keep track of each sister. As it was, he was certain to lose one or the other of them, especially when his attention stayed focused almost solely on June.

June. The more time he spent with her, the more he became convinced they could be happy together, that she was uniquely suited to him. What had Amelia told him once? People had soul mates. He wasn't so certain she was correct about soul mates, but he hadn't met any other woman yet with whom he wanted to spend more time than June.

He stood facing the water under the night sky. A large moon had risen off the horizon and cast a shadowy path of light along the black water. Voices approached along the rocky beach, and Morley was about to turn and make his way back up the Steine when he recognized Annabelle's voice—and a man's.

"Come, Lady Annabelle. We may never be alone like this again."

"Precisely my hope. Now as I've said, I wish to be back up on the Steine. It is not appropriate for you or me to be down here walking out of sight, alone."

"But it could be diverting, much more so." A man's voice, silky, too smooth carried to him.

"I said I'm leaving." Annabelle's voice was firm, but a hint of fear started Morley heading in their direction.

"Not if I say you don't."

"Let go of my arm."

Morley picked up his pace to a run. Very shortly he came upon Lady Annabelle and a man he didn't know.

"Just the lady I've been looking for. How fortunate I should happen upon you right in my hour of need."

"Yes, thank you." She stepped closer to him, the trembling of her hands visible, and then turned back to the man, whose hair was a mess, his cravat disheveled. Morley couldn't place him. Had he met him before?

"Thank you for our walk. I shall finish the rest with Lord Morley."

The man grumbled, "Good evening, Lord Morley." He bowed. "Creeves."

Morley dipped his head slightly. Then he placed a hand over Lady Annabelle's on his arm.

As soon as they were out of earshot, he turned. "Are you well?"

"I hardly know." She stared straight ahead and by the expression on her face, seemed almost unaffected. But, for a moment, before she hid it, her lip quivered.

"Who was that man?"

"He told you. Creeves." She laughed, but it did not light her face. "He's Lord Creevy. He tells people to call him Creeves."

"And he made you uncomfortable?"

She looked away. "I was moving as quickly as I could toward a locale with more people." She stood closer, and her trembling was strong enough he felt it through his jacket. "I assumed him to be harmless, but once we were well away from others, I began to wonder."

"I'm happy to be of service." He turned them back toward the Steine, where others were still out, even at this growing-later hour. They walked for a moment in silence. "How is it you are out without your mother or...who usually chaperones you? Your aunt?"

"My aunt. And she was too tired to be bothered. As soon as we had read together and she began to nod off, I slipped out."

"I think it best if I deliver you back to your place of residence. Where are you staying while here in Brighton?"

"Aunt's apartment. It's just right there, along the Steine."

"Excellent." He led her in that direction. "Surely you know the care you must take."

She lowered her lashes. "I do, certainly. But once a lady has had two Seasons, she starts to wonder if there might be other ways to get married."

"You cannot be serious." He picked up his pace.

Then her voice bubbled up beside him in a humorless laugh, and she stopped walking. "You are the youngest old, stodgy man I've ever seen. Of course I'm not serious. Darling, what woman wants to trap a man into marriage?"

A bit relieved, he allowed himself a smile. "I would hope not you. But there are some who most definitely wish for such a thing. Surely you know the sort."

"And some men who would try to behave abhorrently and then avoid marriage."

"Creeves coming to mind?"

"Yes."

"I guess we both have reason to be embarrassed of our sex."

"Certainly." They arrived in front of her apartments. "I wonder if we might join efforts somewhat during my stay here in Brighton?"

She sidled closer. "You know I welcome any joining that brings me closer to you." Her expression did not hide her interest. It was the boldest declaration he'd heard from her yet.

"What I have in mind does not involve anything romantic between us."

The light in her eyes faded, but she sighed and said, "Understood."

"I will step in when needed, now and again, if you find yourself in the clutches of Creeves or the like. You can help me keep an eye on the Standish sisters—perhaps fill me in on who of the men we see is a man to avoid."

She eyed him, and he wondered if he'd offended her, if she would turn him down flat. But then she smiled so sweetly, relief flowed through him. "I would love the assistance. This is my last effort, my last Season before I go home to our country estate. I have these months in Brighton, and then the wares of London, and then I'm finished."

Morley had his own opinion about whether she should give up. She was a beautiful woman and seemed a decent enough sort. She had a dowry, a good name. She was titled. He wondered what the resistance to her was. Had she turned down offers? Or did no one offer? But he refused to abate his curiosity with even one question. He had enough in the Standish sisters to keep him well occupied on the subject of marriage.

"Will you be joining the group at South Downs Thursday?"

Her eyebrows lifted, but she said, "Yes. I didn't know you would be there."

"Miss Standish expressed an interest."

Her eyes narrowed slightly. "You know you could do so much more with your name and your reputation. You are the most desired Lord this season."

The assessment, spoken in such a financially calculating manner, caught him by surprise. "I'm not sure whether to thank you or cringe."

"Oh, come now. Let's not pretend the thoughts don't cross everyone's minds."

"Thoughts?"

"Certainly. Marriage suitability. We all go through the numbers. Do they meet baseline expectations? And after that, do we wish to look at them fairly regularly? And if the answer to both of those questions is yes, some are satisfied."

"And others?"

"And others are looking for love." Her eyes met his, and the desperate sort of hope that filled them made him sad in a way.

"What if I am looking for love?"

"Have you found it? Or are you so dutiful, so engaged in the task at hand, you've fooled yourself?"

"You forget yourself." He had no desire to abase or wither the tender leaves that had begun to unfurl in his relationship by expressing such things in conversation to another.

She dipped her head, not at all repentant. "My apologies." With a deep curtsy, she said, "I'll see you at the cliffs, then."

At the last sight of her, skirts swishing as she entered her apartments, a small feather of discontent rose inside. Would he regret his newly formed alliance with a woman he trusted only enough to greet in public?

"I see what you are up to here, Morley." Lord Smallwood's voice crawled over him.

Irritation rose inside. "You don't see anything you know a lick about." He turned.

The man stood at his height, eye level, and closer than he expected. "Miss Standish might be interested to learn of your duplicitous rendezvous. Though, from what anyone can tell, you've declared no intentions there, have made no overtures, and Miss Standish's interests might lie elsewhere."

Morley stood taller. "That is a misguided understanding."

"Is it?" Smallwood's eyes flitted to an upper window in the apartments. The curtain closed with a swish, and a shadow moved away.

"Yes, Smallwood," Morley said. "What exactly are your intentions toward Miss Standish?"

"Will you be acting as her guardian? Drawing up the paperwork and such?"

"If she wishes. I or the Duke of Granbury."

Smallwood's eyebrows rose. "Is he still involved?"

"Yes." Morley couldn't bring himself to mention the offer of a dowry for each of the sisters. Perhaps that wasn't fair to Miss Standish, but if things progressed as he hoped they would, he would not have to worry about her future. As long as she would have him.

They stood for a moment more, sizing each other up. And then Smallwood laughed and clapped Morley on the shoulder.

"Come, man. We are friends. Let's have a drink. The others are in the Fox and Stone."

Morley turned to walk at his side. "How long are you in Brighton?"

"As long as it takes, man. As long as it takes."

Morley gritted his teeth but said no more. If Morley had anything to do with it, Smallwood would have to turn his attentions elsewhere or be here for a long time indeed.

Chapter Seventeen

✦❧✦

June had turned down the use of a carriage on their way to the cliffs. Amelia and Gerald would join them in the ducal carriage, walking less, for the sake of Amelia's health. She argued she could manage, but Gerald was adamant. Bless the man. He'd been through so much already in his young life.

But June longed for the brisk sea air and for the vigorous walk. The castle sat inland only a short distance from the cliffs. It stood tall enough she would often watch the sea from any of its south-facing windows, but they had yet to walk to the cliffs. She wrapped her shawl tighter around her body.

"Shall we gather shells for my artwork?" Grace pulled a small bag closer to her side.

"Not on the cliffs, dear." June wrapped an arm around her sister's shoulders.

"Will we not be anywhere near the water?"

"Not unless we walk along the cliffs until we reach a path that leads that direction." Charity joined at her other side. "Which I could be talked into. I long for exercise. All these days caught up inside are enough to drive a person crazy."

"How is your book?" June had heard nothing about Charity's

stories lately, but they had normally been the topic of every dinner conversation.

Charity's frown surprised her.

"What's the matter? Are you still writing?"

"I am." She kicked at the ground in front of them, and June could no longer wonder how Charity went through so many pairs of boots—or slippers, for that matter. "I am to the place where my heroine must fall in love."

"Ooh." Kate held her hands to her face. "Who will she fall in love with? Francis? I do love Francis."

"No, he's too stuffy."

"Thomas, then."

"Too reckless."

"Charles?"

"Too kind."

"Too kind? How can a man be too kind?"

"If he's so kind people steal from him—if he cannot have a backbone to defend himself or his family."

"There aren't any men left in your story."

Charity threw her hands up in the air. "No one is good enough for Cici."

"But can't you write them to be good enough?" June had never seen her sister so distraught about her writing.

Charity pressed her lips together and then shook her head. "No one would believe it. The man who is deserving of our Cici could never exist. He is as fantastical as the Frankenstein creature."

Lucy called from behind. She walked on Kate's arm. "But must she marry someone perfect? No one wants a perfectly boring perfect man."

"And good thing, too, because they don't exist."

"Surely there's one." Charity's eyes turned dreamy, and June would never have believed such a romantic, whimsical expression possible on her sister's face.

"So there's your challenge, Charity. You must write one." June smiled, hoping to ease whatever burdens caused the melancholy on her face.

Grace's voice, quiet at her side, was almost lost to the wind. "Do you think the perfect man exists?"

June thought about her question, and Lord Morley's face came to mind. "I think there can be a man who is just right for us. But overall perfection? None of us is perfect."

"But don't you think a man will seem perfect when you meet him, if he's the one for you? You can't go picking apart everything about a man upon first meeting and expect to fall in love." Kate's expression said she'd given this some thought, and it was a legitimate question.

"I do think a person's faults will become more apparent with time and your immediate attraction to a man can make many a fault seem invisible." June wondered what faults she wasn't seeing in Morley.

"But you didn't like Morley for a long time. I'm not sure you do even now." Grace frowned. "And he's the perfect man."

When Charity snorted, Grace stomped her foot. "No, I really think he is. He's kind and fun and good and is helping us, and he hasn't kicked us out of his estate."

"So that's the measure of a perfect man—one who doesn't kick orphaned women out of their estates." Charity walked faster. "I have yet to see perfection in a man. I have not met one I would deem worthy of any of my dear sisters."

"Someday, Charity. Someday you will fall in love, and you will change your mind," Kate called up to her as her steps became faster.

Then she stopped and turned so suddenly they all had to watch their feet so as not to trip over her. "I should like there to be. I should like to fall helplessly and hopelessly in love, but until I meet a man who is"—she waved her hands around—"who is worthy of such affection, I cannot do it." Then she turned back to the sea.

June considered her sister and once again wondered if Charity's eccentricity would allow her to ever marry. She hoped so, for she could not rest in happiness until each of her sisters was well cared for and happily situated.

At last they made their way across a deep green to the cliffs. The wind picked up. And as they neared an edge, June's heart tightened. "Oh, sisters. It is so high. Please don't go near the edge."

"Are you afraid of heights, sister?" Charity turned to her with mouth open.

"I don't know. I must be. Please, don't go too close to the edge."

"We shall stay far enough away there will be no chance of us falling." Lucy nodded and then glared at Charity, who eventually nodded.

"Right," Charity said.

They walked, June trying not to notice they were up so high.

"Look!" The ducal carriage arrived on the road behind them. Grace pointed and began running toward it, then stopped and waved.

June's eyes trained on the door to the carriage. A footman held it open. June knew the first boot to step out the door. Lord Morley's tall form made her smile, and she had to still her feet from fidgeting in place.

"You are excited to see him." Charity stood beside her. "Is he your perfect man, then?"

"Perfect? The man who won our estate by playing cards?" She smiled, enjoying Charity's answering twinkle in her eyes. "Yes, he just might be." She lifted her arm and waved.

His answering wave was immediate, and it sent her heart into a new round of fluttering. "Oh, oh." She clutched Charity's arm.

Then the duke exited and reached back for his wife. The footman came around with some packages, and each of the sisters tried to see what they brought.

"Is that..." June squinted her eyes and then had to give up.

A carriage pulled up behind the duke's, and several others

were arriving. She trained her eyes down the long dirt road. Many more were coming. This would be quite an event.

The door to the second carriage opened. When June saw Lady Annabelle step out, her heart clenched a little, but she kept smiling, because Lord Morley had moved in her direction with his hand raised.

But then he turned. Lady Annabelle waved to him. He waited for her, and she clung to his arm in what seemed to be an overly possessive manner. And for the first time in June's life, she wished another human harm. Not true harm, but perhaps a little bout of the cold? A soft turn of her ankle? Anything to send her back on her way in her carriage and off of Lord Morley's arm.

She gasped at her own emotion. Was this what happened to a woman in love?

Love? No, she was hardly in love. But she did fancy Lord Morley more than any man she'd met. Her feet stumbled in the rocks. And worse, Lord Smallwood's form hurried in Lady Annabelle's direction from further down the road.

Charity's strength might be holding June up against the wind outside and the upheaval in her heart. "What will we do now?"

"I don't know. Mother never told me anything to do in these kinds of situations."

"And the venerable, ever-present-in-our-conversation Miss Trundle, the governess—she never said anything either?"

"Not at all. Though I don't think she viewed herself as a relationship expert. She was much more concerned with deportment and the manner in which I held my head and my hands"— she leaned closer to Charity—"which seems like completely useless information when put up against my current dilemma."

Both men came closer at around the same time, and she braced herself for another afternoon monopolized by Lord Smallwood, while she watched Lady Annabelle enjoy Lord Morley's attention. But then, as if by some miracle when they were about to reach her, Lady Annabelle released Lord Morley's arm and wrapped herself around Lord Smallwood as though she might never let go.

"Please, Lord Smallwood, keep me safe. These cliffs make me quiver all over. I shall depend upon you."

His gaze flitted to June's, but only for a moment. As a gentleman, he could respond only one way to such a request.

"Certainly." He placed a hand over hers.

Lord Morley arrived at her side in that moment. The air filled with his familiar smell of spice and earth and something else. Perhaps he was using a new soap. She drank it in like she did his smile.

"I'm happy to see you." Her cheeks hurt as though she'd never smiled so large. And perhaps she hadn't. She'd certainly felt few moments of such happiness, and this was all because Lord Morley now stood at her side, when moments before she had thought her day lost to him.

"And I am most glad to see you. And you, Charity, Lucy, Kate —you are looking well. Grace." He dipped a large bow to them all.

Lady Annabelle had already led Lord Smallwood out of earshot. And suddenly, instead of the woman she hoped to disappear forever from her presence, Lady Annabelle had become the beloved heroine of her happiness.

The duke and duchess approached with servants and the packages.

"What have you brought?"

"Those, my dear Miss Grace, are kites."

"Kites?" June had never maneuvered a kite before. "What a splendid idea."

"When we heard of the plan to come out here with the constant wind blowing, Gerald and I knew today was the day."

"Do you carry kites with you in hopes one day you'll fly one?"

"I made some purchases in town." Lord Morley's smile warmed June to her toes.

"Is it very difficult?"

"I shall help."

Others came and gathered around. June smiled at all, even though she'd been introduced to almost none of them. A great happiness continued to grow. Would she at last feel a part of her neighbors? Feel like she belonged?

Lord Morley took the kites from the servants, and she watched while his strong, capable hands attached a string to a large and pointed kite. "And this, my ladies—this is going to soar above us and see sights we never will."

"How poetic." June stood closer. "Will it really fly?"

"Oh, yes. It will go so high we can hardly see it if we let it."

June could hardly believe such a thing possible. But he held the collection of string wrapped around a handle to her. "And you shall be first."

"What! Do you think I shall be able to manage it?"

"Certainly." He stepped closer so only she could hear. "The wind does all the work, and I'll help."

"Let's do this then, shall we?"

He wiggled his eyebrows. "Can we clear a space?"

The group which had gathered around backed away, and Lord Morley stepped toward the road with the kite in hand. The string unwrapped from her hands and followed him. Then, once he was a certain distance away, he called, "I'm going to let go. You back up a bit when I do."

"And that's it?"

"This beauty will fly. Trust me."

She watched the sparkle in his eyes, and she knew she did. She trusted him. "I'm ready."

Lord Smallwood and Lady Annabelle joined the group, watching their kite experiment. Lord Smallwood whispered something to her, and she smirked.

"Are you ready?"

June's eyes returned to Lord Morley, and she nodded.

"On my count. One, two, three!" He threw the kite into the

air, and she stepped back, pulling on the string. It whipped higher, almost yanking the string out of her hands.

She screamed and laughed and called out, "Oh, you did it! You're flying! Go, go, go! Higher!" She no longer cared who heard or who saw; she was so caught up in the freedom of the kite.

The string flew from her hands, the handle spinning, until Lord Morley murmured, "That's high enough. Hold tight."

"Oh, oh, yes." She held it taut and felt the tug as the kite jerked from side to side way up in the air. "This is incredible. Thank you."

"My pleasure." His breath warmed her neck. He stood just behind her, almost close enough that she could shift her weight back upon him, close enough his body warmed hers. He reached an arm forward so she felt almost wrapped in an embrace. He steadied her hand. "Allow me. This can be tiring."

She nodded, hardly breathing, wanting his attention to continue, now, forever. "I feel connected to the heavens. This is wonderful." She turned to him and became almost immediately overwhelmed by his closeness. His warm eyes sparkled down at her. His strong arm encircled her, his hand steadied her own.

The line jerked. "Oh!"

The kite started swaying back and forth in the sky.

"May I?" He offered to take it from her.

"Certainly. What has gone wrong?"

"Oh, nothing. This is quite normal. The air is not steady or predictable up there." He started winding as quickly as he could and pulling the kite in closer.

June stepped away to give him some more room, but as soon as she did, he turned to her. "I will perform much better with you at my side, I assure you." Then he winked and waited.

Laughing, she stood again as close as before.

"That is much better. Thank you." His murmur rushed through her in great, happy waves. Was this what it was like to be in love? If so, it was lovely.

Soon he pulled the kite close enough that it once again bobbed nicely in the sky.

"Might I try?" Grace stepped forward.

"Certainly." Lord Morley waved her over, and then June knew she must make room. He caught her gaze once more and then turned his attention to Grace.

Kate and Lucy were both lost in conversation with different small clusters of people, and for a moment, June didn't know what to do with herself. She looked wistfully out to the ocean. A part of her longed for more of the walk she had been on with her sisters. But their pleasant solitude couldn't last all afternoon, nor should it. With a sigh, she turned back to the group.

Lord Smallwood stepped up to her side. "And how are you this fine afternoon?" He bowed, as gallant as ever.

Lady Annabelle was making her way to Lord Morley on his other side.

"I'm fine."

He eyed Lady Annabelle attaching herself to Lord Morley's other arm. "Shall we allow him to do his duty?"

"Pardon me?"

"And woo the woman of his mother's choosing?"

June looked from Lord Morley, who was in what looked like a pleasant conversation with Lady Annabelle, and back to Lord Smallwood. His smile was large and sincere. But she didn't say anything. Although she doubted very much Lord Morley would ever show such a preference for herself if he were intended for someone else, a part of her wondered. And that bit of wondering had great power to shake her confidence.

Chapter Eighteen

L ord Morley helped Grace keep the kite steady.
When Lady Annabelle linked her arm to his, he
smiled. "Thank you for your timely rescue. A particular
gentleman was waylaid for enough time that today has been
productive."

"Productive?" She wrinkled her nose. "How unromantic."

"I shall keep all romantic sentiment for the person it is most
meant to impress."

She lifted her chin. "You have an avid competitor in Lord
Smallwood. And I feel a part of her is at least considering his
suit. She is to respond to him by the ball."

"Respond? In what manner?" He looked from Smallwood to
Miss Standish and back. They seemed friendly enough, perhaps
more on his part. Was she enamored with him? Surely not. She
would not be as accepting of his attention if she was planning on
receiving that of another. But had she been accepting or merely
friendly with him? When moments before he had been so sure
of his progress, Morley was now plagued with doubt.

Lady Annabelle laughed under her breath. "And the venerable
Lord Morley shows his uncertain side. Come now, we will make

our plans." She meant to pull him away, but he shook his head, surprised.

Then he turned to Grace. "Have you met Lady Annabelle?"

Grace turned her beautiful blue eyes to Lady Annabelle. "I believe we have met. It's good to see you again." Grace curtsied. "And you as well."

"Lady Annabelle is going to be helping us through the Season here in Brighton."

"Helping us? How?"

"Oh, just helping me know which men to introduce your sisters to, helping me keep an eye on them at the balls and things —those kinds of important tasks."

She didn't look convinced, but she smiled. "That's nice. Thank you."

"You're welcome, of course. Lord Morley and I are close... friends." She smiled up into his face, and for a moment, Morley wanted to peel her arms off of his. But they had an agreement, and so far, she'd been nothing but helpful.

They finished their kite flying. Grace left his side to talk to others. As soon as the kite was once again on the ground, Morley looked around. All five sisters were in sight. He breathed out in relief.

"They will be fine. What could happen out here in the open like this?" Lady Annabelle laughed.

"I don't know. But even these men—some of them I wouldn't leave them alone with the sisters. Weatherby, the others."

"Weatherby?" Lady Annabelle scoffed. "He's harmless."

He had taken Grace to look out at the ocean view. Grace was laughing and seemed to feel comfortable.

"I've never seen him so attentive. Perhaps you're right. He has a harmless helpful side."

Two men approached, each with Kate and Lucy on their arms. "Lord Morley, we were wondering if we might come call."

The first man placed his hand over the top of Kate's. "Are you the one to petition with such things?"

Lady Annabelle nodded, but whatever she was about to say was lost.

June joined them. "You would need to make those kinds of petitions to me." She glanced at Morley. "And him, if he would like, but I'll be the one making the decisions."

The men shared a look, and one smirked. "Tomorrow, then?"

"Yes, June. We've invited them for a tour." Lucy looked at the others who stood near. "We could have any who would like. The castle renovations are worth seeing. The portrait hall is still intact. The armory, some of the statuary hall." Lucy smiled. "And the turrets. They've completed work on the turrets and towers."

June smiled. "We'd love to have you. Please come any day during normal calling hours."

More guests were taking their leave. The duke led his wife toward the carriages in a slow, careful manner. Perhaps these outings were too much for Amelia. Then they all made their way to the carriages. Lord Smallwood handed June up, and Morley handed up all the other sisters.

As soon as the carriage doors closed and the horses began moving, Grace lifted her feet and leaned back on her carriage bench. "That was amazing."

Morley grinned. "Did you like the kites?"

"Lovely." June's smile filled the carriage and Morley with a new form of sunshine. "I don't think any of us has had such a pleasant afternoon."

Even Charity looked pleased.

"I did see each of you with a different gentleman...or three." He laughed at Charity. "Any of interest?"

"None yet." Lucy sat with her ankles crossed and her chin high. She looked like a well-trained debutante.

"I don't think we need be so particular." Kate swished her skirts. "There was a time we weren't certain we would ever marry."

June placed a hand on her arm and gave it a soft squeeze. "Very true, sweet. My wish is simple: I want for you to be happy and cared for. Whoever it is you find who makes that happen will be the one we support." She looked to Morley as if to seek his agreement, and his chest filled with air.

"Precisely. We care most for everyone's happiness."

She reached for his hand. "And I have some news."

"Oh?" Morley searched her face. "What is it?"

"We may have made some progress in discovering the story behind the jewels." June grinned.

Morley had almost forgotten the jewels. "Does anyone else know of them?"

"They are safe in my chambers. But I have consulted with someone to determine their worth, and it could be great indeed."

"Why, that's wonderful news." Morley frowned. "But perhaps, if that's the case, I should give them to the bank?"

"To be deposited in your account, no doubt." Charity crossed her arms.

"Certainly. What account should I put them in? They are the estate's jewels."

"But Morley, the letter said they were for us." Grace's eyes were filled with uncertainty.

He considered her words. "Too true. It did say that, didn't it?" He turned to June. "Have you learned more about them?"

"Perhaps. Some books in a chest in what must have been a library have been a fascinating resource."

"I imagine so. I'd love to search them with you."

"Perhaps tomorrow we could."

"I'd like that." Morley wanted the jewels to be the sisters'.

They stared into each other's eyes until Charity cleared her throat.

June looked away. "But what I did find was mostly just what we already know. We are descended from the Normans. From William himself. He charged that this castle be built and the land be cared for by his brother. And it was his wish the land remain in the family."

Morley nodded. "It is so fitting the renovations are underway, that you are once again to live in the estate of your forbearers."

June squeezed his hand in hers. "We may not know immediately or even soon, but I do think if we persist, one day we may know the full story of our family."

Morley looked from one to the other of the sisters. They had become as dear to him as real sisters ever could be. "What if the castle holds greater secrets? What if there is more here King William would want you to uncover?" His smile grew as he thought about it. "I feel its secrets might not be known now or all at once, but one of the meaningful things about this castle is it might be trying to tell us something through messages left. What say you?"

"What a perfectly romantic and adventurous thing to say!" Kate shifted in her seat. "Perhaps we can skip lessons tomorrow to go seeking what more could be hidden here."

"In our free time only." June closed her eyes. "The dresses and the alterations come tomorrow."

"Save a dance for me?" Morley said the words without thought. They flowed out as the most natural desire of his heart, which of course it was. He wanted nothing more than to dance every dance with her, at every ball, forever.

"Which would you like?"

"The first and both supper sets."

She laughed, and the musical sound flowed through him. "I shall save those sets for you."

"Excellent. And if I might dance a set with each of my sisters?"

Kate giggled. "You can have any of my sets."

"I'll save you my third." Lucy's face was calculating, and Morley was amused. For all her seeking an increase in her station, he knew her heart to be golden. He'd seen her caring for the tenants down the street from the cottage.

"I'll save a set for you." Grace acted as though perhaps they would forget she could not attend. And for a moment, looking into her deceptively calm face, his heart softened.

"Could I have your fifth?"

Her eyes widened, but she said only, "Certainly."

June frowned, but said nothing. He shrugged in return and planned to give it some thought.

They arrived shortly after the duke. His carriage was being stored and his horses cared for when Morley and the sisters pulled into the front drive.

"I hear talk of fine stables," Morley said.

"Oh?" June's voice gave away her excitement.

"Yes, with some of the finest horses of even the London set. Many stable theirs here."

"I'd love to see them."

"And so you shall. Perhaps we can go tomorrow or later this week."

As he watched her face, drinking in the pleased expectation he saw on it, Morley realized he could spend many a day, hour, or minute doing nothing but working to make her smile.

He exited the carriage and handed down each of the sisters. The others went into the house, but Miss Standish lingered.

"Thank you for today. Again—I am always thanking you."

"And you mustn't, for I'm selfishly motivated."

The corner of her mouth lifted. "Are you?"

He brought her hand to his lips. "Most definitely."

She sucked in a breath, her eyes widening. "I look forward to the ball. We all do."

"And I'm scared half out of my wits."

She laughed. "You needn't be. We will have their graces, you, me. The sisters will be fine." She paused. "But Grace..."

"I know. I shouldn't have agreed to a set."

"But now you have."

"Could she attend with Amelia? Dance with only me? Be a companion of sorts?"

"Perhaps, if you think it wise."

"Shall we think on it? I find I cannot make any more of these sorts of decisions tonight. I want nothing more than to tuck your arm in mine, enter this lovely castle, read for hours by the fire, and never leave your side." The thought warmed him, as there were other things he'd like to do. Her full mouth puckered and then softened in pleasure as he was talking, and he was tortured by it.

"I should like nothing more. Will you return tomorrow?"

"I shall. I have some correspondence to attend to, and then I will arrive before any callers. Tour the castle, did they say?"

"Oh, yes. I had forgotten."

"Have their eyes been caught by anyone in particular? I confess I cannot tell."

"I don't think so. Not yet."

"And have yours?"

Her cheeks flushed, and her eyes lowered, but then her smile grew, and she lifted her lashes, stepping closer. "My eyes have been caught, yes."

She stood close enough for him to pull into his arms, to press his mouth on hers. His arms ached to do so, and his lips tingled with the anticipation.

"Anything else?" he said.

"My mind." She placed her hands on his lower arms, her fingers pressing, calling him to close the distance. He teetered, rocking forward. She lifted her chin, her eyes searching his face.

"And your heart?"

The nod started small, subtle, but it grew, and her eyes sparkled in a new confidence. "I think so."

His own heart skipped, his mind whirling with happiness. His arms wrapped around her, his mouth yearning for hers. "I—I cannot resist much longer. Might I—might I kiss you?"

Her hands went up his chest and wrapped around his neck. He pulled her closer, and then his lips covered hers, their softness sending thrilling waves of pleasure through him. She was everything. Her kindness, her selfless love for her sisters, expecting nothing from life but giving everything. He didn't think he could ever love a woman more.

More—all he wanted was more, but he stopped. He paused in the delicious exploring of her mouth. "June." He closed his eyes and breathed. "Might I use your name?"

She nodded and then giggled. "And am I to call you Morley? Have you another name?"

"Nicholas. But even my mother calls me Morley."

"Then I shall as well, except for certain moments, like now, when you will forever be my Nicholas." She lifted her chin and kissed him. "Nicholas."

"I shall never hear my name the same again." And then he grinned.

And she grinned and started to laugh. She held a hand to her mouth. "I'm sorry. I'm just so happy."

"As am I. Might I call tomorrow?"

"Yes, please. Every day."

He bowed to her with one more kiss upon her hand. "Until then, I will be counting the moments."

He got in his carriage, filled with happiness that he was now courting Miss Standish. She stood with a hand in the air until his carriage had rounded the bend from her house. And then he sat back on his bench, a smile permanently etched on his face. He'd write his solicitor tomorrow. The marriage papers and settlement must be drawn, and he thought he knew what she might appreciate as a wedding gift.

Chapter Nineteen

The sisters all gathered again on June's bed.

"I think I'm getting married." She giggled as she said it, and Kate and Grace screamed. They hopped off the bed and danced with each other around the room.

Lucy nodded with approval. "Lord Smallwood is the most sensible choice. He is titled. His family comes from—"

"Smallwood? No. It's Morley, of course." She looked from Lucy's face to the others. No one else seemed surprised.

"I'm sorry. I knew you had feelings for him, and he seems to have them for you, but you are both so studiously entertaining Lord Smallwood and Lady Annabelle I naturally assumed, regardless of your feelings, you were moving forward out of duty or some other motivation."

The sisters all stared.

"It would not be the first time a woman—or a man, for that matter—set aside love to make the sensible choice, and our June and Morley are both nothing if not sensible." She stopped, as no one responded. Then she shook her head. "But I see I was mistaken. You have my fondest congratulations."

"Did he propose?" Charity hadn't said anything yet, and her face was not readable.

"Well, no." June considered their interaction.

"Did he declare his love?"

"Um. No." Was she assuming things?

"Then why do you think you will marry?"

June looked away, embarrassed to speak of such things. "Well, because..." She glanced at Grace and then back at Charity. "We kissed. He seemed—I assumed—oh, dear. Do you suppose he is not going to propose?" She pulled off her gloves and placed her cool fingers on her flushed cheeks. "Do you think he is the type of man to kiss a woman, to seem so enamored, and then not propose?"

"Certainly not." Kate shook her head. "Not our Morley."

"But in truth"—Charity frowned—"we don't know what type of man he is when it comes to the ways of courtship and marriage." She huffed. "What if he is the type to kiss many and offer to none?"

June felt the blood drain from her face, and she fell to the edge of her bed. "Surely not."

"Charity, stop. You're upsetting June." Grace sat at her side. "I'm sure Morley is sincere in his attentions. You'll see. He will propose, and we will all be the happiest of sisters."

"I can only hope, but you'd best be prepared for the worst." Charity reached for her hand. "I know I sound unkind, but I speak with the best intentions. I just want to see that he backs up his actions with an offer. Otherwise, why would he be kissing you?"

"Yes, sweet. I know you do. We haven't had many evidences of the goodness of fate, have we?"

"How can you say that?" Kate shook her head. "How can you say that when you look around you?"

June amended, "Yes. You are right—so very right. Sometimes when I focus on all we have lost, I forget all we have gained." She smiled through a new mist in her eyes. "And I wouldn't trade it, not one bit." She reached out her arms. "Come here, you."

They all moved in and hugged June as best they could. She

threw her arms around the lot of them, and the fierce love of sisters was almost enough to dull the new ache their worries had caused. No matter. If it turned out Morley was uninterested, or his duty lay elsewhere, or he changed his mind, she would weather the storm as she had all others. She blinked back her tears, squeezed them all one extra-strong squeeze, and then said, "Now, off to bed. If I don't fall into mine, I shan't be able to entertain all the men begging for tours of the place."

Kate squealed. "Oh! It's true. She's right. Let us sleep." She rushed from the room but paused in the doorway. "I love you, sisters. I shouldn't like to live this life with anyone else." She almost left, then poked her head back in. "Up until now. I imagine a husband wouldn't be so bad in the future." With a giggle, she ran down the hallway.

For many hours, June sat at her table near the fire. She ran her fingers along the books in her nearby bookshelf. *Aladdin*, Faust, *The Marquis of O, Pride and Prejudice, The Tales of Shakespeare*, a collection from Byron. Like old friends, just the sight of them cheered her. She thought back over her moments with Morley—Nicholas. The smile tugged at her mouth. He cared for her. He must. Perhaps he hadn't immediately thought of marriage as she had, but he was pursuing her. He had more than just a friendship in mind, surely. And that was good enough for now. June smiled. He'd called her by her first name. She ran her fingers lightly over her mouth, reliving the sensation of his mouth, his murmuring endearments, his soft lips sending tingling all through her. She'd been overwhelmed with emotion. Had he continued, she might have fainted dead away. She laughed. And how would that have looked?

She readied for bed and fell asleep.

Even when she woke in the morning, the pleasant happiness, the ready smile, and the warm and tender feelings remained. When just one month past she had resigned herself to only book friends and a warm fire for the rest of her days, she now had a man in her life who had captured her heart and showed such love for her sisters. She didn't know how she would ever be happier.

The sisters prepared themselves in such a pretty and happy fashion June wasn't sure how any man was not to fall immediately in love with each Standish. When she thought of their hearts, their compassion, their intelligence, she could not be more proud of her sisters.

As soon as it was remotely appropriate to accept callers, Lord Smallwood stood at her door. He was announced in the front room. All the sisters stood, and every face looked at June.

She smiled. "Lord Smallwood. How good of you to call."

"I heard we are having a tour of the castle this morning?" His smile was warm. He seemed in good spirits. June wondered what he would say when she told him she'd made up her mind, and he was not to be courting her.

"We are having a tour as soon as the others arrive. Would you care to sit down? We have tea and coffee, as well as some cakes." She indicated with her hand an empty chair.

"I wonder if first we might have a moment? Perhaps we could take a turn in your side gardens?"

"Oh, certainly." She swallowed. She knew this would be the best moment to explain to him she was not planning to consider his courtship. How could she when her own heart was so engaged elsewhere? She could not string him along as a second choice. Some women might consider such a tactic, but marriage as a prize was not even a good enough reward to treat another human so.

She nodded to her sisters. "Do greet our guests as they arrive. I shall return shortly."

In the hallway, she paused in front of a footman. "Would you please see that one of the servants accompanies us outside?"

"Yes, miss." The footman nodded and moved away.

"Thank you for letting me pull you away from your sisters and from the normal calling time."

"I hope we will not be too long, as I must assist. You understand."

"Of course. We seldom get a moment between us. I had hoped just for that—a moment."

Her heart twisted, for what she was about to say to him would not leave her lips easily, nor would he be pleased to hear it. Instead of delaying what must be said, she stopped him in the hall near the entrance. "Lord Smallwood, I have come to an understanding and a decision."

"Have you?" His eyes lit, and his face glowed with happiness, his mouth slower than the rest. But before it could grow, she shook her head.

"I cannot accept your courtship. I cannot."

"You're refusing me before I can even try? Before I can court you properly?"

"I am." There was nothing more to say. She tried to soften her words. "I have been honored by your attention. You were the first to show any interest in me, the first to notice, and I have appreciated knowing you. But my affection remains unengaged, and I seek for more than friendship in a marriage."

"And can you afford to be so particular? Could our friendship not grow into something more?" His words were pleading, but his eyes had taken a new glint to them, a harder, steely expression.

"I do feel I can be as particular as I would like. I know our friendship could grow, yes. I do not wish to take that step to find out." She put a hand on his arm and stepped closer, looking into his eyes, hoping he would understand. "I know you will find happiness, more happiness, with another."

A noise behind them startled her, and she spun around. Morley had entered, and his expression was unreadable. An older woman stood next to him on his arm. Her face was pinched and her chin lifted in disapproval.

June dipped a quick curtsy to Lord Smallwood and then

hurried toward the entry. "Lord Morley. You have come." She held her hands out to him.

But he only took one, his other engaged by the woman on his arm. He bowed over hers and then said, "I would like to present my mother, Lady Morley. Mother, this is Miss Standish."

June's heart skipped. "Oh, hello! Hello, Lady Morley, and welcome to our home." She waved a hand toward the entry. "Do come in. We are expecting many friends today, for we've offered a tour of the castle."

"*Your* home? I am pleased at my son's magnanimity that you can feel so at home here."

Ooh. Something about the comment stung, a reminder of how beholden she was to Morley. "Yes. He is all goodness and kindness."

Lady Morley's eyes narrowed as she seemed to take in all of June at once, the tiny tear at her hemline, the scuff marks on her slippers, the tip of her hairstyle.

June tried to hold on to her courage. She grasped at every bit of confidence she could muster from deep inside. Morley was not helpful. His face still wore a mask. Gone were the warm, affectionate expressions from the night before.

"Will you join us? I'd love to introduce you to my sisters, if I may."

"There are five of you, are there not?" Lady Morley's voice managed to be disapproving and polite at the same time.

"Yes."

"And you are the eldest?"

"I am."

She sniffed.

June had no way of knowing how to interpret what she could mean by it, but she pressed forward anyway. "We are so pleased to have you here. I am certain you will enjoy the recent renovations to the property. It is a splendid addition to the Morley estate." A part of her heart twisted to say it. She had almost begun to think of the castle as theirs, with the discovery of the jewels and the note. In actuality, June owned nothing—certainly not the castle, her only possessions some gowns and books and their parents' things she hadn't sold.

"Morley has told me much about the renovations. Perhaps *he* can do me the honors. I suspect you must see to your guests." Her gaze flicked to where June and Lord Smallwood had been standing.

June turned to see and was grateful Lord Smallwood no longer stood in the hallway. "The others can take care of our guests. The conversation you interrupted was finished. I was clearing up a misunderstanding." Her eyes pled with Morley's for understanding.

His nod was slight, but it warmed her with a large dose of relief. "Let us go meet the Standish sisters, Mother," he said. "I enjoy them all—a delightful family I'm happy to know."

"Very well."

Morley led his mother on ahead of June. Oddly, he didn't offer his other arm to her. What was going on? Had she disappointed him? Had he kissed her and his interest ceased? Was she a terrible kisser? Such a thing had never occurred to her before. Was his mother opposed to their match?

That was likely. She seemed a disapproving sort of person. And Lord Smallwood had warned her the woman had her own plans for Morley. June's hands were unsteady, so she clasped them behind her back.

The footman opened the double doors. "Lord Morley, Lady Morley."

Everyone in the room stood. None of the gentlemen had yet arrived, for which June was grateful. While Morley introduced his mother to each of June's sisters, she moved to stand beside Charity, whose face was full of questions. June could only shrug.

Their servants brought in more tea. Bless them. June listened in confused silence while Morley and her sisters maintained an awkward conversation.

Lady Morley replaced her cup on a saucer. "And who has taught you all? Trained you in matters of deportment?"

"June did, my lady." Grace smiled. "She's taught me to dance, to read, all the arts, literature, the major poets. I can compute, hold a book on my head for twenty paces, play the pianoforte, and sing." She waved her hand around. "And more things I cannot remember at the moment."

"And how does Miss Standish come to know all of this? Were you a governess, then?"

"Oh, no. I had one. And I retained much of what I learned so I could pass it on to my sisters."

Lady Morley looked her over again. "And these gowns— they are lovely and of the finest material. How came you by them?"

"Mother." Morley dipped his head.

"I am simply making her a compliment."

"We thank you. This particular gown was given to me by the Duchess of York."

Lady Morley's eyes widened, and her eyebrows rose into her hairline.

"Am I to understand you receive the Duchess of York?"

"And the Duchess of Sussex. She said she would visit today, in fact." Charity's posture was bold, and she was tapping her toes. June knew it wouldn't be long before she said something off-putting to Lady Morley, and the more the woman talked, the more June wished she would.

"You didn't tell me that."

"I must have forgotten. It seems today is the day for visitors."

The footman announced. "Her Grace, the Duchess of York."

The sisters gasped, and in walked the Duchess of York. "Oh, my lovelies. My dears! I hear the Duchess of Sussex has come to call." Her shrewd eyes flitted over the group in one quick movement. "But I see you are wearing my gowns. Sensible of you. I do enjoy gifting them and appreciate when the recipients are grateful and make use of the gift."

The occupants of the room curtsied—or bowed, as was the case with Morley.

June stepped forward to greet Her Grace. "You do us a great honor. And you have found us in our new place of residence. What do you think of the castle?"

"It is lovely. Do you suffer from the cold here? Unless you have the finest materials, castles can be terribly drafty."

"Thank you for your kindness. We are doing what we can right now to try to alleviate some of that."

"I shall have more tapestries sent over. They're the best thing, really. Coming from the north, I know what to do for the cold and the drafts."

"We would be most grateful, Your Grace." June turned. "Have you yet met Lady Morley or the Earl of Morley, her son?"

Her Grace nodded, eyeing them, then held out her hand to Morley. "Yes, we have met. I'm pleased to see you again, Lord Morley, and your mother."

June almost laughed when she merely nodded in Lady Morley's direction before moving to sit next to June.

"Tell me, Miss Standish. How is the social situation? Any improvement since I last visited?"

"Oh, much has greatly improved, Your Grace. And I do wish to pass on just how many of the people we see compliment us on our gowns."

She nodded, an expression of great satisfaction crossing her face.

The footman again stood in the doorway. "Lords Kenworthy, Tolleson, and Foxwood here to see you."

The sisters stood.

The lords who walked in full of pomp and overconfidence faltered a moment at the sight of Lady Morley and the duchess. Then they promptly stiffened and bowed low. "Your Grace. Lady Morley, Miss Standish." Lord Kenworthy rose from his bow, and the others followed suit.

"Callers! How lovely." The duchess leaned over conspiratorially to June. "How pleasant to have callers. I do believe it's the new gowns. They look so fine on all of you."

"Most assuredly." Charity leaned forward and spoke around June, which Her Grace did not seem to mind.

"Miss Charity, how is the book you are writing?"

"I have hit a place where I don't know what comes next."

"That's very nice, my dear."

June wondered if she'd heard anything Charity said at all.

"So, has the Duchess of Sussex been by? I heard she has."

"She has." Charity nodded, her eyes sparkling.

"And did she leave more things?"

"She did. We were ever so grateful. So many lovely things."

Her Grace shifted in her chair. "I hope you will enjoy what I have sent as well." Once the sisters all nodded and exclaimed about how much they would appreciate her generosity, she turned her gaze about the room. "And you gentlemen."

The lords sat forward, and one, Lord Kenworthy, laughed, "Yes, Your Grace?"

"What are your intentions here with these women?"

Kate sucked in her breath.

But before anyone could answer, the footman entered and said, "The Duchess of Sussex here to see you, misses."

Everyone in the room stood.

She swept in, her skirts swirling about her, and a footman followed with several more boxes of things. She waved for them to be placed back against the wall. The room grew smaller by the second.

"Hello to all. I see Minerva is here." She air kissed the Duchess of York and then did the same with June. The duchess nodded, but only briefly, to Lady Morley.

June forced herself not to smile, but it was with great satisfaction she watched Lady Morley be soundly snubbed by the royal duchesses. Perhaps Lady Morley treated everyone in an off-putting manner.

Morley hadn't looked in her direction many times. And June

realized no matter what the duchesses thought of Lady Morley, if her son respected her wishes, June would never be with her son unless the woman approved.

The Duchess of Sussex made herself comfortable on the other side of Morley, and June moved to pour her some tea.

The duchess patted her hand. "You are such a dear. You always make it just as I like it."

"Thank you, Your Grace. You honor us by your presence and your gifts."

The Duchess of Sussex smiled, her eyes full of shine and happiness. Then she looked in the Duchess of York's direction. "Did you bring gifts as well?"

"I did indeed."

They both seemed to size each other up.

The footman announced yet another group of arrivals, and June remained standing as more men from their kite-flying outing stepped into a room which could no longer hold them all. June clapped her hands. "Perhaps now is the perfect time to begin our tour. We've asked our new housekeeper, Mrs. Holling, if she would lead us, and, of course, the sisters will accompany. Your Grace, and Your Grace, would you like a tour of the castle?"

"I think I would." The Duchess of York stood, which encouraged the Duchess of Sussex to do the same.

Morley led his mother from the room. All the sisters followed. And June would just as soon have stayed in the front parlor to meet any of the other callers, but she saw Lord Smallwood once again lingering in the front area of the home, so she followed the group on their tour.

Chapter Twenty

Morley wanted nothing more than to have just a moment with Miss Standish alone. He had immediately thought wrong of her. The sight of Smallwood in a private conversation with Miss Standish had set his blood to boiling.

But as soon as he'd stood near her for but a brief moment, as soon as he'd seen the gracious manner in which she'd responded to his mother, he knew he'd overreacted. But he couldn't behave in a normal fashion with his disapproving mother on his arm. Her pinched face and murmuring comments put a damper on everything.

Mother's hand gripped his arm. "Why are all of these people here?"

"They are friends of the Standishes, Mother. I told you a tour had been planned."

"I cannot fathom so much interest in an impoverished family."

"They are distant relatives of the royal house." He adjusted his cravat, wanting his mother to understand. "And they have dowries now, and the castle of Northumber. They are in much higher demand than you would think."

"Very distant. And living at the mercy of others—*your* mercy."

"That's not the way I choose to see it."

"Everyone who has eyes will see it that way."

"But what would be wrong for any of these good men to marry a woman of the royal house, no matter how different, who has a dowry, was raised in a gentle life, and has excellent connections?"

His mother looked away. "If you mean by 'connections' the duchesses who compete about the charity they give, I hardly call those 'connections.'"

"They are more highly connected than I." He led her further away so no one would overhear. "And I am interested in their affairs. I wish them success. Miss Standish especially is important to me."

His mother stiffened. "Well, I see nothing wrong with you helping them to marry. They will more quickly be out of your house. Miss Standish is a pretty enough girl. She will find a good man, though likely no one of the nobility, who could marry much better."

"You're not seeing clearly. She's magnificent—"

Lady Annabelle joined them in that moment. "I didn't know Lady Morley had come. It is so good to see you." Lady Annabelle curtsied, and his mother reached for her hands. "It is good to see you too, my dear. I was just telling my Morley here about the merits of marrying well."

Lady Annabelle's eyebrow rose. "Were you? And I missed it? I think I should find such a conversation very entertaining."

Lady Morley nodded. "You, for example. You're such a lovely girl."

"Oh, you speak too highly of me." She linked arms on his mother's other side. "I'm not much different from anyone else."

They caught up to the rest of the group, and Morley caught bits of a conversation between the Duchess of Sussex and Miss Standish.

"A luncheon will be just the thing," the Duchess of Sussex was saying. "If you wish it, I shall let your cook know the specific instructions now."

"I think that is a wonderful idea. And not to worry about talking to Cook. I shall do so. I know what has been purchased recently, at any rate."

"Very good, dear." The duchess looked impressed, and Morley's heart grew in pride.

Then Gerald and Amelia joined them.

His mother frowned. "And now we are to be set upon by that shopkeeper girl."

"Mother, she is the Duchess of Granbury."

"But some of us won't forget her birth. Or the scandal of her parents."

"And why hang onto something so trivial and unrelated to your own life and happiness?" Morley was just about ready to leave his mother alone and let her fend for herself.

He would have raised a hand in greeting and moved to converse with his best friend, but for his concern about his mother's vitriolic tongue. And then there was the situation with each of the sisters. Who was watching each of them and their interactions?

June returned at that moment and clapped her hands. "Might I say a word?"

Everyone quieted.

"We would love for you all to follow me into the dining hall for a bit of luncheon. We know it isn't always done, but you are all here and are so good to come for a tour of our home. And we would love to offer a bit of something."

From the general increase in noise, the idea seemed to be received with favor. They moved to the room just outside the dining hall.

Gerald bowed to the Duchess of York, Amelia at his side. "Might I have the honor of escorting Your Grace?"

She dipped your head. "And might I wish the two of you every happiness? From Frederick as well."

He bowed, and Amelia said, "Thank you, Your Grace."

Lord Smallwood bowed to the Duchess of Sussex. Morley's eyes rose in surprise, and his gaze met Miss Standish's. He stepped in her direction, but his mother tugged on his arm.

"We should be next," she said.

"Yes, and I am going to escort Miss Standish."

"You will do nothing of the kind. What will people think?"

"Hopefully they will think accurately that I admire her."

Lady Annabelle hid a smile with her hand, but her eyes flashed, and Morley couldn't tell what emotion played across her face. Then he realized he'd be leaving her without an escort were he to offer his arm to Miss Standish.

Instead he dipped his head. "Forgive me. I didn't want the hostess left alone, but in so doing, I would be neglecting my duty here."

"So dutiful." Lady Annabelle's victorious smile scratched at a tender place inside. When she came to his other side and latched onto his arm, he fought against a strong desire to peel her away.

Miss Standish followed with Lord Weatherby, and the man had already engaged her in pleasant enough conversation that she was laughing.

Gerald took the head of the table with Amelia on his right. Morley sat at the other end with his mother on his left. He pulled out a chair on his right. "Miss Standish?"

She lifted her eyebrows, and then Morley almost cheered when the slight pink dusting of her cheeks told him she was pleased. Perhaps she'd forgiven his less-than-warm greeting when he arrived. Lady Annabelle sat at his mother's side and then Smallwood at her side. He could have hugged Charity for sitting at Miss Standish's other side.

The luncheon was expertly presented. Servants delivered a

simple fare but in a most pleasing manner. The Duchess of York was beside herself in praise.

"I commend your idea to have such a luncheon. And the sandwiches are as fine as any I've had. Well done, Miss Standish. I knew I bestowed my friendship on a most worthy woman."

"Thank you."

"The sandwiches are somewhat stale in reality. I would think you could do better with the Morley estate staff." His mother sipped her wine. "But for a woman who has never had such a responsibility on her shoulders before, I agree. The luncheon is nice."

Through smiling teeth, Miss Standish whispered, "Was that a compliment?"

He murmured in Miss Standish's direction, "That's as complimentary as she gets."

"Thank you, Lady Morley. Thank you, Your Grace."

The group chatted for the rest of the luncheon. Morley only partly listened to anything except June until the guests finished and began to depart.

When his mother was finally ready to leave—she insisted they outstay both duchesses—he helped her step up into the carriage, closed the door, and turned back to Miss Standish, who stood on the front stoop to bid them goodbye.

He stepped as close as he dared, lifting her hand to his mouth. Then he pled with her, "You were wonderful. Lunch was amazing. I couldn't be more pleased. My mother...she...are you well?"

Her eyes held as much insecurity as to make him want to encircle her with his arms and kiss away every worry, but instead he waited.

"I think I am well. Your mother..." She sighed.

"Don't let her worry you. I'm Lord Morley."

"Of course I'll worry what your mother thinks of me."

"You will? Does it matter to you?"

She looked down, her lovely lashes lining her cheeks. "It matters a great deal."

And that sweet response would have to sustain him, to sate his urge to pull her into his arms again and kiss her senseless. "Will I see you at the ball?"

"First set and supper."

"And every other moment?"

"Every moment it would be proper..."

"So I must share you with others?"

"You must, but I wish it weren't so." Her cheeks colored pink again.

"Until tomorrow, then. I shall leave before I forget myself in front of my mother and give her something real to pinch her lips in disapproval over."

She gasped. "You wouldn't."

"I wouldn't—yet. But there might come a day." He winked, then dipped his head and stepped away.

As he climbed into the carriage, his mother shook her head. "Someone has to save you from making a fool of yourself."

"If I am making a fool of myself, I happily do so. No saving necessary, Mother."

She said nothing more, but he knew he hadn't heard the last on the topic.

Miss Standish stood at the front door to their marvelous castle until his carriage turned the corner.

Chapter Twenty-One

⁂

June stood at the bottom of the stairs, waiting for her sisters. She'd never felt so beautiful in a dress. To wear something specifically and perfectly fitted to her was a luxury she'd never been afforded until now.

The duke and duchess entered the main foyer area. Amelia hurried to her. "You look lovely."

"Oh, thank you. Thank you so much for these gowns. I had no idea it would look like this. I feel like"—she tried to blink away moisture from her eyes—"I feel like"—she spun—"I feel beautiful."

"And you are. Inside that giving and lovely heart as well as outside." Amelia embraced her. "We shall be here, awaiting the stories of your successes."

"I could never thank you enough for all you've done for my family."

"Think nothing of it. Thank your uncle's cousin, who passed away and gave the properties to me." His Grace chuckled.

Energetic chatter alerted them to the arrival of each of the other Standish sisters. Lucy descended first, then Charity, followed by Kate. Of them all, Kate's dress seemed to reflect light, it was so stunning.

She approached, out of breath. "This is the most amazing night of my life." Charity wore green, and it suited her better than any other color. Lucy was in maroon, and June's dress was blue. They'd all opted against the debutante white. It wasn't their Season. They were simply attending a ball they'd been invited to.

Grace descended last. Her pink dress was a modified ball gown. It better suited a younger girl. But she still looked beautiful and every bit as appealing as the other sisters.

"Are we certain you should come, sweet?" June looked to Amelia.

"I am certain I should come." Her lip started to protrude, but she pulled it back in. "I will be careful. I will dance with no one but Lord Morley and will stay in sight at all times."

"Well, that sounds just fine." She looked around at them all. "Are we ready? I think my sisters will be the loveliest women at the prince's ball."

Charity linked arms. "Shall we?"

"We shall." June turned to the front door. The clinking noise of a carriage, the stomping of horse hooves, waited outside. She turned back to the duke. "Thank you for the use of your carriage."

"You are quite welcome. To all of it. Though I do think Morley was a bit disappointed not to be fortunate enough to lend the use of his."

"But then we'd have to ride with his mother." Charity made such a face, and June found it so diverting she could not scold her.

The footman handed them up one at a time. With their gowns, the fit was more snug than last time in the carriage together, but June couldn't stop the smile that stretched across her face. "I wish I could paint us all like this, so I might remember this moment forever."

Charity squeezed her hand. "I think you are the closest of all of us to finding true happiness."

"Do you think I've found love?"

"Do you?"

"I think so. I am truly very happy, sisters. I wish the same for you."

"I hear there might be many others at this ball, people from Town and friends of Prince George." Lucy's eyes lit with hope.

"And those we are to avoid. If possible, we shall avoid an introduction to any of Prinny's set." June studied their faces. They seemed as excited as she. "But most of all, let us enjoy ourselves. And Grace—"

"Yes, I know. I mustn't dance with anyone but our Morley."

June smiled at the mention of his name. Morley. Was he to be *her* Morley? She clasped her hands together because she didn't know what else to do with them or the energy that coursed through her. "To think, we are at last included in a ball." Her feet tapped under her skirts.

They stopped in front of the Royal Pavilion, and even though June had seen it many times from a distance, the entrance alone was far more grand than she had suspected. The bulbous structure with the spindles rose up all around her. The front double doors, gilded, gold, and brilliant, were opened, and the royal servants, in red livery, lined the entrance.

As soon as they stepped inside, the later-afternoon, early-evening light shone in through the stained glass ceiling to give everything an ethereal pink glow. The walls were lit by hanging lanterns, and the stands were wrapped in dragons, snakes, and leaves. Bamboo seemed to grow from the walls. Soldiers from the orient guarded as statues on either side.

The sisters were speechless until at last Charity murmured, "I didn't know Prince George had such beautiful taste."

"Frederick Crace is his chief decorator, but I hear the prince had particular requests." Lucy's eyes were wide.

The corridor was long and wide, and June walked slowly. Though she wished to arrive at the banquet and looked forward to the ball, the corridor alone gifted her with much to view, much to appreciate.

"I've never seen anything so beautiful." Grace clasped her hands together.

They followed the line of people ahead of them through the palace, taking in every space, each room more elaborate than the next. June peeked into what was described as the music room and paused in the doorway. Dragons, in what looked like gold, intertwined along the top walls. The deep, rich reds and golds and warm yellows combined to draw the eye in every direction.

Charity tugged at her arm. "Perhaps we can come see more later?"

"I do hope we can, for these sights must be seen," June said in a hushed voice.

Eventually they were led toward what must be the ballroom, for the sound of the Master of Ceremonies calling out the names of the guests carried over to them.

When they reached the entrance, June pointed out their names on his list. He announced, "Miss June Standish, Miss Charity, Miss Kate, Miss Lucy, and Miss Grace."

Some in the room paused to turn in their direction.

June looked out over the swirling dresses, the colors, the lovely blue-colored walls, the statues of dragons, the tall replicas of Chinese palaces, and she smiled. And then her gaze connected with Lord Morley's, and she didn't see anything or anyone else. He approached from the center of the room, making his way around and through the clusters of people.

Music began as the instruments were tuned, and June knew they would be calling the first set soon.

Loud laughter startled her, and a group of boisterous lords surrounding one overdressed and overweight man walked by.

"Prince George," Lucy whispered.

June nodded, grateful not to claim an acquaintance with him or his friends.

Lord Morley bowed at her front and reached for her hand. "I believe we have this first set."

She curtsied low. "Yes, we do." She turned to Charity. "Would you find a place for Grace to sit and care for each other?"

But several other of the lords they'd entertained at the house yesterday bowed over her sisters' hands, and she knew they would soon be out on the floor dancing. She searched the room, and then her eyes stopped on the Duchess of Sussex.

"Do you suppose?"

Lord Morley followed her gaze and then nodded. "I'm sure she would be happy to assist."

And he was correct. Her Grace patted the chair at her side and introduced Grace to all the older ladies who sat near.

Then Morley led June out onto the floor. He smiled and saw only her. When he bowed, his eyes searched her own. When she tiptoed around him, the air between them drew her closer. The longer they approached and then backed away, almost touching but not quite, grasping hands but only for a moment, the more she wanted to slip her hand in his and run off somewhere so they could be alone. She wanted his eyes only on her, his arms around her, and, she was embarrassed to admit, his lips once again caressing hers. She hardly dared think such things, but the desire came unbidden. When she passed him next, her cheeks heated, and he winked. She gasped once she'd passed him. Could he read her thoughts?

But when their dance ended, she wished it would begin again, for Lord Morley dropped her off with the duchess and went in search of Charity, who he'd secured a set with next. Before he left, he'd pressed his lips to her fingers. "The supper sets and a very long dinner in between will be ours."

She pressed her hands to her stomach as he walked away, knowing no matter how long the prince's elaborate meals, it would seem too short.

The evening progressed. Lord Smallwood claimed a set. He was polite. Lords Kenworthy and Tolleson both came to ask her to dance. Her sisters seemed equally engaged and happy, even Grace. The last June had looked in her direction, a number of the older women were laughing at something she'd said.

At one point, June was without a partner and went in search of a drink. Her lips were parched, and she felt overly warm. Lord Morley had asked Lady Annabelle to dance, and it was the waltz.

As she stood at the lemonade tables, dabbing her neck with a handkerchief, Lady Morley surprised her. "You've been enjoying yourself, I see."

"Oh, hello, Lady Morley. It's good to see you."

She pressed her lips together. "Do you really feel yourself equal to my son?"

June almost spit out her lemonade on the woman. A part of her wished she dared. "Pardon me?"

"Will our estate have to bear the entrance and blood of one so unworthy?"

"I'm sorry, but I'm sure I don't know what you are talking about." June hoped most fervently she was not expressing such open dislike of the idea of a proposal from Morley.

"Do you really think your wiles have so fully entrapped him his own mother won't have sway? That someone as beautiful and worthy and titled as Lady Annabelle won't have an influence?" She waved her hand at the smiling couple waltzing.

"I don't have any thoughts about any of those things. I'm sorry, if you'll excuse me—"

"You will not leave me. I am not finished. Lady Annabelle is meant to stand at Morley's side. She is the one worthy of such a title. Do you think I could become dowager to the likes of you?" She scoffed. "Soon he will see. Very soon he will notice how unprepared you would be for such a task. Managing an estate such as the Morley earldom? Do you even know what that would entail?" She shook her head. "You don't."

June swallowed, fighting tears. Why was this woman attacking her so? "I'm unsure what I've done to make you dislike me so—"

"Done? You haven't *done* anything. You aren't anything. If my son were ever so fooled as to agree to a marriage, he would be immediately and sorely disappointed as soon as you attempted to do anything necessary to act in your station and purpose as his wife."

Her legs shaking, she placed an equally trembling hand on the table at her side. Then she turned from Lady Morley without another word. Rushing from the room, she almost ran into Lord Smallwood.

"Oh, excuse me."

"Miss Standish? Are you ill?" His hands held her shoulders. "You're trembling. What can I do to help?"

"Nothing. I must leave this room."

"Certainly." He kept an arm firmly across her shoulders, and she wrapped her arms around her own middle, holding herself up. How could someone be so cruel?

He led her out to a verandah, and as soon as the cooler air washed over her in a gentle refreshment, she felt better. He handed her a handkerchief. She wiped her eyes, dabbed her neck again, and then attempted a smile.

"Thank you. I am feeling better."

"Lady Morley is a force to take on all by oneself. I'm surprised Morley left you to her."

"He's dancing. I don't suppose he knew it was happening."

"I saw him leave the floor with Lady Annabelle on his arm."

"Oh." She didn't know what to say as her emotions took a turn for the worse. "Well, then, I don't know."

'Don't you?" He raised an eyebrow.

"No, I really don't." Before she could stop herself, large tears fell from her eyes. "Oh, dear." She turned from him.

But he came to her, turned her back and pulled her close. His hug felt nice, undemanding—caring, even. "There. Don't let anything that happens at a ball disturb you in such a strong fashion, especially not at one of the prince's balls. All will be right tomorrow."

But she'd thought Morley cared. Of course, he cared! She was being silly. His mother had shaken her. But if his mother hated her so, would he ever really seek her hand? Yesterday she thought there might be a chance at winning her over, and now she knew it to be impossible. Would she marry a man and divide him from his mother?

Perhaps he would never seek her hand. He'd said nothing about it yet, though he'd kissed her. Doubt crowded her mind, and her legs started shaking anew.

"You're trembling again." Lord Smallwood ran his hands up her back. Then she stepped away, and he put his two hands at the side of her face. "Look at me."

She lifted her lashes. His eyes seemed sincere.

"You are worth ten times Lady Annabelle. You would make any man happy. You—"

Giggling interrupted as Lady Annabelle clung to Morley's arms, draping herself across him, exiting out on the verandah near them. He laughed. "Lady Annabelle, you are a wonder. What can I do to thank you?"

She tipped up on her toes, inches from his face. "Kiss me. Kiss me like you used to."

"What!" June couldn't stop her outburst.

Morley looked up. Annabelle turned. Lord Smallwood tightened his embrace, and Morley frowned.

"What is going on here?" Morley's tone was harsher than she ever remembered it being, and something about the injustice gave her courage.

"I wondered the same thing," she said.

"If you'll excuse us, Morley, this verandah is taken." Lord Smallwood's tone also bothered her.

"Oh, stop," June said. "You act as though we need a moment alone." She pushed him away.

"It looks to me like you do," Lord Morley said.

"And you as well." She waved her hand at Annabelle, who still clung to him.

"You have no idea what you're talking about."

Annabelle giggled.

"Don't I?" June said.

He gently unwrapped Annabelle's arms from around his neck. "No."

"Well, it looked to me like I misunderstood your intentions."

"If anyone is misunderstanding things around here, it's me," Morley said.

"Precisely." She crossed her arms.

"Wait. That's not what I meant."

Lord Smallwood laughed. "Tell us. What did you mean?"

"You're not helping, Smallwood."

"Oh, believe me, my lord. His intention is not to help you." Annabelle's giggle raised the hairs on June's arms.

Then three of the Standish sisters rushed out onto the verandah, Charity in the lead, Kate and Lucy wringing their hands.

"Grace is missing."

"What!" June and Morley shouted together.

June ran to her sisters. "What has happened?"

"No one knows. Her Grace said she was aching for a lemonade and a nice gentleman offered to get her one. She turned back to Grace after a moment, and our sister was gone."

"Who was the gentleman?"

"We're trying to determine that right now."

"What has been done?" Morley's strained voice, the urgency in his questions, comforted June more than further worried her. She was not alone. Even if she was devastated he could not be hers, at least he was dutiful.

He and June ran back to the entrance to the ballroom. June searched the faces, and Charity stood at her side. "She's not here. We checked the women's room, everywhere, the libraries. There are so many places she could have slipped off to with all manner of disrepute."

"I know." June felt her panic rising. "I know all that. What do we do?" She hated that she did, but she turned to Morley. "What can be done?"

His eyes had narrowed, he nodded to her, and then pushed through the room to a small corner of men. June followed, the sisters right after.

"Where's Weatherby?" Morley stood close to Lord Kenworthy. The man stepped back, his gaze flicked to the sisters and then back to Morley. "At the stables, most likely."

Morley turned and ran.

"Wait!" June called after, ignoring the few people nearby who were paying attention to their crisis.

Smallwood followed as well. As soon as they'd left the ballroom, he called, "What are you doing, man? That's what a magistrate is for. Don't bother yourself with this."

June gasped, praying Morley would ignore him.

"Are you daft? I go myself. She's my sister." He dipped his head once to June and then ran away from them all, down the hallway.

Charity swung her reticule at Lord Smallwood's shoulder. He rubbed his hand over the spot where she'd hit him and then turned away. "She's ruined you all now."

"Wait." June ran to him. "You will keep this quiet for now, won't you?"

He was about to shake his head, but after a moment, he sighed. "I'll keep it quiet. No promises about Lady Annabelle, though."

June turned to her sisters, a great, sick worry building up inside. She held her arms out, and they rushed together in a great embrace. "I hope everything will be alright."

"Morley will take care of it. I know he will." Kate nodded against them.

June hoped she was right. "I don't think I care to be here at this ball any longer."

The girls nodded. They made their way around the ballroom, back toward the front door, and called for their carriage.

The line of carriages stretched a long way. The line of guests waiting was equally long. They were going to be standing there a long time. While they were waiting, Kate hugged June tightly. "I know he loves you, June. I've seen it in his face."

June wished her sweet sister was correct.

Chapter Twenty-Two

June and the sisters arrived home to a quiet house. They said little. June's heart broke with every quiet breath she took. They moved as one, their steps slow, toward their parlor sitting room. One of the maids approached and curtsied. "If it pleases you, miss, Lord Morley is in the parlor with the misses."

June's heart jumped out of her throat. "What! With Grace?" She took off running, tearing down the corridor and through the door into their parlor.

Grace lay on the couch. Morley pulled a blanket up to her chin, and his expression was soft. He placed a hand on her forehead. Grace's eyes were closed. Then he wiped his eyes and stared at the ceiling. The pain etched in his face tore through her, and her love for him magnified. No matter how he felt or who he loved, she loved him. This pain he felt for June's family, this love he showed them, was worth more to her than anything.

She hurried to his side.

He startled, wiped his eyes again, and then pulled her into his arms. "June, my June."

She rocked in his embrace.

He kissed the top of her head. They stood thus while the sisters gathered round, each one seeing for themselves Grace was well and truly home again and on their couch. Then June became vaguely aware that Charity shooed the other sisters from the room.

When they were alone again, except for a sleeping Grace, June stepped away and searched his face. "Tell me what happened."

He led her to the other side of the room, and they sat on a sofa together. "Nothing had come of it, though Lord Weatherby is a snake among men. I don't trust his intentions at all."

"But where were they?"

"He'd taken her to get a lemonade and then talked so much of Prinny's horses he'd convinced her to go see them. When I got there, a horse was being saddled, but they were talking only with stable hands all around."

"Oh, thank the heavens." Her hands shook in relief. "I was so worried."

"I as well."

"I saw your face." June reached out and laid a hand on his cheek.

"Were you standing long enough to witness my agony?"

She nodded. "I can't believe you love my sisters so much."

He shook his head. "I do love them, but that pain was for a different reason."

"Was it?"

"Yes. That pain was all for you."

Their moments on the verandah rushed back to her, and she looked away. "Oh."

"And I cannot bear this misunderstanding between us, this distance. You in Smallwood's arms. Tell me at once, and please, don't toy with my heart. Are you in love with him?"

She sucked in her breath and then shook her head. "No. I am not." She studied his face.

The great relief that smoothed all his lines and brought a

light to his eyes told her much. But she had to know, to hear from his own mouth, a number of things.

"I spoke with your mother at the ball tonight."

"Oh?" His face turned wary.

"Yes, and she most thoroughly and completely disapproves of me in such strong terms I was certain you could never care."

He frowned. And then he stood and began pacing in front of her. "She has no business..."

"And then I saw you dancing with Lady Annabelle, and she was in your arms. She is your mother's first choice, would be a perfect Lady Morley, and so on. I cannot stomach repeating all her words."

He stopped.

"I was in tears. What you witnessed was Lord Smallwood comforting me."

"What *you* witnessed was some form of subterfuge between Smallwood and Lady Annabelle."

She started to shake her head, then paused. "Was it?"

"I can only guess. She literally dragged me out there and acted as though she'd had way too much to drink. She draped herself all over and suggested we kiss."

When June stiffened, he shook his head.

"No," he said. "She and I have never kissed. And that is how I know she knew you were there. She lied and put on a show for someone: you. And I suspect it was Smallwood who led you there. How was Smallwood so available to comfort you right when my mother was uncharacteristically harsh?"

"Uncharacteristically?"

"Well, certainly. She's unkind. I know that. Most women keep their distance from her, but to approach you at a ball and say horrible things to your face, when she knows she would be taking a personal risk because of your friendship with the duchesses—when she knows she might be overheard? This was planned."

Her heart lightened just a little at his assumptions but then tightened again. "But if what you say is true, she well and truly does not want me in her family. And Morley, I don't know if I can continue our relationship if your mother feels this way."

Morley held up his hands. "Please, say no more. For a moment let me say all the words which must be said. For there are many still begging to be released from my hesitant heart."

At the word "hesitant," June worried. But she nodded. "I'm listening." Her voice sounded small even to her ears. She held her hands in her lap and waited.

Morley stopped pacing and came to sit beside her. Then he stood again. But he was soon at her side again, sitting. "I'm not very good at this."

She wanted to laugh, but he seemed tortured, so she said nothing.

"I don't know where to begin. So I'll start backward, with my mother." He lifted her hand and placed it in his own and then began toying with her fingers. "I do not wish for you to think me an uncaring son. But it is my plan to send my mother to the northern estate and ask that she tend to it—and *only* it—for the rest of her days."

"What!"

He winced. "I do not want to sound uncaring. But she will not be needed. And she will cause more damage than good with whomever I marry. I am working very hard to find a woman nothing like my mother to spend my life with, and I would just as soon the woman's influence had no sway on my life, estate, or future relationships."

Astounded, and perhaps a bit giddy, June just nodded and tried not to smile overly large.

He chuckled. "So, mother out of the picture. Now, Lady Annabelle." He shook his head. "She has offered herself to me a number of times, and every time I have refused. I am simply not interested in Lady Annabelle."

His eyes were full of sincerity and honesty. June studied him for a moment. And she chose to believe him.

"She doesn't seem to make you happy in any way."

"No, she absolutely does not make me happy in any way." He pulled at the tips of her glove. "And that brings me to the next thing I hope to express to you in just the right way, but I'm having the most difficult time of it. Perhaps if I just begin, it will help."

"Begin what?"

"Begin telling you how I feel." His face turned red, the deepest red, and June was astounded. Could Morley have a shy side? She would have never guessed. "When words matter the most, they fail me. But I shall press forward. June—my dearest June. Almost immediately upon seeing you in that little cottage, I..." He continued to tug at her glove, but it wasn't coming off. "This confounded thing. Why won't it leave your hand?"

She laughed. "You just have to be patient with it. Tug gently, one finger at a time." She pulled at her index finger, then her middle, until each finger was loose, and then he took over, pulling the glove and freeing her hand.

"Much better."

As her bare hand was enveloped in his, every sensation in her body responded. Tingles ran up her arm. Her mouth went dry. Words escaped her. As her eyes widened, she couldn't believe something so simple as Morley holding her bare hand could have such an effect.

"I will continue. I have been completely lost to you from the moment of my arrival here in Brighton—happily so, I might add."

June smiled, feeling her courage rise. "Lost to my charms? My wiles? My entrapping you, as your mother would undoubtedly accuse?"

"No, none of that. Lost to your beauty, your mind, your heart, your goodness to your sisters, your persistence in the face of everything against you, your loyalty, and..." His eyebrow rose, and the hint of daring made her grin. "And your lips."

"Ha!" She laughed. "My lips!" She looked over her shoulder.

Grace's eyes were still closed. "That is what your mother would call my feminine wiles."

"Be that as it may, they are nothing of the sort, as far as I'm concerned. They are a homing beacon to my tired heart, and I long for you whenever I am not near."

"Beautiful words."

"Perhaps I'm better at this than I realized. I shall continue to practice more on you until one day you shall proclaim me a poet." He left the sofa and lowered himself to one knee. "But this next part I can only say on my knee. For I feel so unequal to the goodness in you, and yet I come before you as I am. I love you. You have my heart, my mind, my life, if you want it. I pledge to love you until my dying breath—with the hopes you will agree to marry me?"

Tears filled her eyes. "Oh, Morley—Nicholas. I love you, too. I have loved you from the beginning. Yes, I will marry you. I shall do my best to be worthy of you and to stand at your side in all things." She lowered to her knees in front of him. "You are everything I never thought would ever happen to me but secretly hoped would. Thank you. For coming here, for discharging your duty so well, and then for loving me in spite of it all." She put both hands on either side of his face and pressed her lips to his.

He wrapped his arms around her, responding immediately. He pulled her closer. Her hands went up into his hair. She fell against him in such a way he almost toppled over backward. Chuckling, he reached a hand out to steady them against the sofa. A great yearning rose up inside, filling her with longing, with adoration for Nicholas, with a desire to never leave his side. It clenched and pulled, and she pressed more insistently back in response to his kisses.

He groaned and then he paused. "My June." He kissed her once more. "I must stand. We must marry at once so I never have to bid you farewell again."

"The sisters might want a big wedding."

"No, we shall not. We just want you married so Morley can come live with us at last."

They turned to Grace, who was sitting up with the largest smile on her face. "And congratulations." Her smile turned impish.

June thought her face would never cool from the fire that raged across her skin.

"Then we must tell everyone. Wake the house!" He jumped up, tugging on June, and ran out to the courtyard shouting, "Everyone! Everyone! We have news!"

Doors opened. Feet ran down hallways. And soon every other Standish sister stood along a balcony railing, looking down upon them.

After a moment, a disgruntled and tired-looking Duke of Granbury joined them as well.

"We're getting married!" Morley clapped. "June has agreed. She loves me."

"Very good." The Duke of Granbury's smile grew. "I'm happy for you, cousin." He dipped his head to June. "And for you. If you can put up with his quirks, this here is the best of men."

"Thank you, Your Grace."

"Gerald," he mumbled, but then he turned from them. "Morley, sleep here tonight. Take the room next to ours."

"Capital idea." His smile could only grow.

The sisters clapped their hands, and then Grace raced upstairs.

When alone again at last, Morley pulled June close and kissed her one more time, which left June yearning for more, and then sent her upstairs to join her sisters.

As she looked down over her shoulder, he stood, arms crossed, his gaze falling over everything around him with the most satisfied expression she'd seen on a man. She paused, studying him, and knew with this man, she would be very happy indeed.

***

Read Book THREE in the Lords for the Sisters of Sussex Series. Click HERE.

The Duke's Second Chance Chapter One

The duchess's labor had started in the carriage while returning to their London townhome. Perhaps her pinched face and general malaise during the earlier parts of the day should have clued the duke in that all was not right, but she gave no complaint, and now he was left only to wish she had expressed a word or two of her condition. He'd carried her himself into her room, her gowns wet through. At last on her bed, he was relieved she would be in the hands of someone more experienced than he who knew how to care for her. But as he brushed the hair from her forehead, as he gazed on his beloved's face, he couldn't bear to part, not yet, not with her in the utmost misery.

Gerald clasped his wife's hands in his own, hoping the strength of his love for her would scare away the pain.

Her face pinched, and she doubled over, large drops of sweat falling off her forehead. "Don't leave!"

"I'm here. Our illustrious midwife will have to unleash her dragon claws on me before I leave."

That brought a tiny laugh from his wife which gratified Gerald to no end. He tried to keep up a form of banter with Camilla who was clenched in the pains of childbirth, but in truth, if she wasn't gripping him so tightly, everyone in the room would see the trembling in his own limbs. She cried out. "It's getting worse. Is this supposed to happen?" Her eyes, wide with terror, made him frantic.

"Someone do something!" He had tried to find his deep barreling voice but the order came out more of a squeak than anything.

The midwife sidled up to him, "Pardon me, Your Grace. If I may?" She attempted to separate their hands, but he and Camilla resisted, gripping tighter. She continued, "She is doing wonderfully. Her body is performing just as we would expect it to. Everything is progressing as it should. Soon you will have a new baby."

Camilla rolled toward him onto her side, moaning and writhing on the bed.

"If I might?" The midwife gently tried again to pry their fingers apart, but Camilla clung to him. "No." Her no came out as a long drawn out syllable and he almost stepped back in fear. But her grip on him offered no mercy, and no movement.

"I'm here." He stated his determination to remain at her side. Though even to himself, his tone sounded less sure.

He hesitated one more moment, then Camilla screamed as though she were on a torture rack and released his hands, clutching instead the soothing cool fingers of their midwife, her cooing tones soothed Gerald as much as Camilla.

Gerald scooted further away. The door opened behind him. "Your Grace. I came as soon as I could."

Gerald turned. "Dr. Miller. Thank you for coming."

The doctor held the door open for him. "I'm presuming you were on your way out?"

Gerald nodded. "Yes, quite." Just for a moment he would step into the hallway.

His wife turned eyes to him, beautiful, shining eyes full of love. "I shall be finished shortly they tell me." Then her body clenched again and she curled into a ball. "Make it stop. Please make this stop."

"I love you, Camilla."

She waved him away, clenched in apparent agony.

The doctor shooed him out the door and before it closed firmly behind him, Gerald heard a quiet, "I love you too." Gerald leaned up against it, breathing heavily. What a daft thing to do, impregnate his wife. What in the blazes was he thinking doing such a thing to them both? He closed his eyes, her scream audible through the thick door.

"Oh this will not do." His friend's voice lessened the strain that wound inside Gerald like a tight net.

Gerald whipped his eyes open, a welcoming smile interrupting the pain of his moment. "Cousin Morley. I've ruined her. She'll never forgive me, I'm certain, and she's in the most incredible pain."

Another scream interrupted. The door flung open and a maid ran out, carrying linens and a bucket. The door shut firmly after her.

Morley gripped his shoulder. "Come, man. This is not the place for husbands. Wives always seem just fine after it's all over."

"I don't know. She seemed determined I stay by her. I'm taking a break." He swallowed.

"No, they say that at first, but what woman wants you to see her like that? It's only going to get worse. You should have seen my sister's household. The whole place was in a upheaval, everyone thinking their lady was going to fire them all."

Morley considered his friends words. "And when it was over, she was recovered?"

"Certainly. She was in the best of moods, gave them all an increase in pay." Morley put an arm across his shoulder. "Come. We don't belong anywhere near her. It's off to the study with your fine brandy."

Gerald nodded. "Indeed. That sounds like just the thing." He hesitated a moment more and then allowed the good will of his dearest friend to lead him along to a brighter manner in which to pass the time.

The farther away from her bedroom, the more the fibers of worry lessened, and Gerald told himself his wife was in the best of hands, that women gave birth all the time and that surely she would be well. He pushed away a persistent, niggling worry that something terrible was happening, pushed it as far as he could. For just as his friend said, what more could he do? She would be well soon enough and he could meet his son or daughter. Their lives would continue as before.

Morley made himself comfortable in the study as he always did. Leaning back in his favorite chair, he said, "Remember when we convinced Joe that his cow was about to give birth?"

Gerald snorted, almost losing his mouthful of brandy. "Clueless Joe believed us, with not a bull in sight on their estate."

Morley laughed and raised his cup in the air. "To Joe."

"To Joe."

They downed their cups, and Morley poured two new ones.

"Thanks for being here."

"Would I miss the best thing you've ever done?"

Gerald eyed him with suspicion. "That sounds very sentimental..."

"We hope. If your child is anything like *Her* Grace, then we're sure of you doing a service to society..."

"And if the child's like me?"

"Then we've just inflicted society with another Campbell, and I don't know how I feel about that."

"Being a Campbell yourself."

"Precisely. I know what a pox we are on the land."

Gerald downed his second cup, grateful for a reason to laugh. "Tell me cousin. Will there ever be another Campbell in your life?"

"If my mother has anything to say on the matter."

"And what say you? Surely someone has caught your eye?"

Morley looked away, his face drawn in an uncharacteristic

frown. "I've found women to be nothing more than a silly, grappling means of entrapment." He coughed. "Present wives excluded."

Gerald sympathized with his friend. Finding a woman to marry should not be so difficult. He felt supremely lucky, blessed, in his marriage to Camilla. They had fallen in love straight away, both of them happy to pursue a courtship, their parents pleased, society approving, but he knew it wasn't so easy for most people.

"Come, man. I shall devote the next bit of my life to making you the happiest of men."

Morley held up his hands and shook his head. "Assistance not necessary. In fact, quite unwelcome."

"Think nothing of it. I want you just as happily situated as I am, for marriage has brought nothing but the best of feelings. Today's activities aside, naturally."

A man cleared his throat in the doorway.

The doctor, at last. Gerald rushed forward, shaking his hand. "Are you the first to congratulate me?"

Morley arrived at his side, his face pinched.

The doctor looked tired, older by ten years since he'd arrived. "Your Grace."

Alarm spiked through Gerald. "What is it? Camilla? Is she well? The baby?"

Dr. Miller shook his head. "We could have never known the baby would be sitting backward, that the duchess would bleed like she did..." Dr. Miller rubbed his head with a shaking hand. "I'm sorry, Your Grace."

Gerald grasped the man by the shoulders, trying to clear his mind, trying to shake the brandy from his cloudy thinking. "Speak sense man."

"We lost her." The words left the doctor's mouth in a slow motion, his face falling into a sick despairing expression.

"What?" He turned from Dr. Miller and ran to his wife's bedroom, his heart willing the doctor's words to erase. Holding his breath, wishing to erase the last hour. He pushed open the door, a maid falling to the floor on the other side as he rushed to his wife's side, lifting her frame into his arms, her sickly white skin still warm to his touch. He clutched her to his chest. "Camilla."

Her arms hung limp at her side. He lifted them, holding them close to his chest. Her neck drooped, her head hanging uselessly at her shoulders. "No." He lifted her head so it was upright. "Camilla. Can you hear me?"

Someone stood at his side. And a familiar hand clasped his shoulder. "Gerald."

He shook his head.

"Gerald."

He clenched his eyes tight, blocking out the world, blocking out Camilla's lack of response, blocking out the friend at his side, even the doctor's words.

And then a cry broke the silence. A baby's cry.

Gerald's eyes fluttered open, and his heart pounded. Turning his head, he clutched Camilla tighter. A baby cried in the arms of their midwife. He could not make sense of this infant. Why was there a baby in the room making all that racket? Didn't they know that his Camilla needed help? He blinked, trying to understand what he was seeing. Morley stepped to the side of the midwife and took the child into his arms. "Looks like you have an heir."

And then everything seemed to speed up and race past him. And he made sense of his situation. "Take him out."

"Pardon me, Your Grace?" The midwife seemed hard of hearing all of a sudden.

"Out. Now. I don't want to lay eyes on the creature who was the cause of Camilla's death."

"Oh, but surely this slip of a thing had nothing—"

Morley placed a hand on her arm, shook his head, and the woman wisely held her tongue.

Then Morley said some nonsense about the nursemaid

before it was once again blessedly quiet. He released Camilla's dear body and placed her precisely the way she liked to sleep, on her side, with one hand under her cheek. Then he pulled the blankets up to her chin and tucked her in carefully. He was surprised by the tears that fell from his eyes, wetting everything. His body shuddered, his breaths coming with great effort, fighting against a new tightness that filled his chest.

He stood, unsure what to do. Did he stay by Camilla? Yes. He sat back down. But what more did she require of him? She was at rest, the ultimate rest. He stood. Who took care of such things? Her burial. Someone had to let Camilla's parents know. He covered his eyes, the wetness there again surprising him.

"Gerald."

Morley stood at his side.

Gerald turned again to his oldest friend. And the man who stood a hand taller than him, pulled him into his broad chest and hugged him like a young lad. And Gerald clung to him until his body quit shaking. Then he stepped back, at last able to take in a full breath. "What is to be done?"

"I'll take care of it. We'll notify everyone who must know. We will make arrangements for her burial."

Gerald turned away. Camilla already looked so far away. Her lifeless form had nothing to do with the vibrant soul who used to inhabit it. The light that had shone through her eyes, that broadened her smile, the laugh that had started deep in her belly and bubbled overflowing into a great and joyful music...everything that made Camilla who she was, was gone. And Gerald didn't know where she went. He reached down and placed his hand on her forehead, seeking the last bit of warmth left, finding precious little, he whispered, "Goodbye, my love, my dearest Camilla."

And allowed Morley to lead him out of the room.

READ the rest of this story HERE.

Follow Jen

The next book in the Lords for the Sisters of Sussex.
Her Lady's Whims and Fancies

Jen's other published books

The Nobleman's Daughter
Two lovers in disguise

Scarlet
The Pimpernel retold

A Lady's Maid
Can she love again?

His Lady in Hiding
Will her Charade cost her the man that she loves?

Spun of Gold
Rumplestilskin Retold

Dating the Duke

Time Travel: Regency man in NYC

Back to His Lordship
Time Travel. She goes back to Regency.

Charmed by His Lordship
The antics of a fake friendship

Tabitha's Folly
Four over protective Brothers

To read Damen's Secret
The Villain's Romance

Follow her Newsletter